"Jenna! Where a

"Sean? Help!" A faint c̶—̶—̶ inside, followed by a fit of coughing. "I'm trapped."

Sean pushed the door wide and darted inside. Smoke assaulted him immediately. His lungs burned. He snatched the dish towel that lay on the countertop near the sink, turned on the water and saturated the cloth, then covered his mouth and nose with it.

"P-p-please...h-hurry," Jenna choked out in a raspy voice.

He darted through the cased opening to the dining room. He willed his vision to adjust, but the haze of the smoke was working against him. "Where are you?"

A deep hacking cough answered him. "Here," she said. "On the floor. Against the wall. Between the sofa and the side table."

He mentally visualized the layout of the room. "Closest to the dining room or the entry hall?"

"Entry." Another scratchy cough. "The fire is on both sides of me. There were two Molotov cocktails thrown."

Two? Whoever did this had meant to cause the most damage possible.

Sirens pierced the night. Help was on the way, but he knew he couldn't wait for them to get here.

He had to get Jenna outside. Now.

Rhonda Starnes is a retired middle school language arts teacher who dreamed of being a published author from the time she was in seventh grade and wrote her first short story. She lives in North Alabama with her husband, whom she lovingly refers to as Mountain Man. They enjoy traveling and spending time with their children and grandchildren. Rhonda writes heart-and-soul suspense with rugged heroes and feisty heroines.

Books by Rhonda Starnes

Love Inspired Suspense

Rocky Mountain Revenge
Perilous Wilderness Escape
Tracked Through the Mountains
Abducted at Christmas
Uncovering Colorado Secrets
Cold Case Mountain Murder

Visit the Author Profile page at LoveInspired.com.

COLD CASE MOUNTAIN MURDER

RHONDA STARNES

LOVE INSPIRED SUSPENSE
INSPIRATIONAL ROMANCE

LOVE INSPIRED® SUSPENSE
INSPIRATIONAL ROMANCE

ISBN-13: 978-1-335-98041-0

Cold Case Mountain Murder

Love Inspired
22 Adelaide St. West, 41st Floor
Toronto, Ontario M5H 4E3, Canada
www.LoveInspired.com

Printed in Lithuania

And the Lord, he it is that doth go before thee;
he will be with thee, he will not fail thee,
neither forsake thee: fear not, neither be dismayed.
—*Deuteronomy* 31:8

This book is dedicated to Jackie Layton,
Cate Nolan and Dana R. Lynn. Thank you for being
my accountability partners and for helping me stay
motivated and on track as I completed this book.
I couldn't have done it without you.

ONE

Jenna Hartley folded her hands on the round table in front of her in the tiny bedroom she'd turned into a home office that she used for a podcast studio in her East Tennessee home and leaned forward, as if making eye contact with her listeners. "That's all for today, folks. Thank you for tuning in to *Seeking Justice with Jenna*. Tune in next time, when we discuss the Boxcar Killer trial, shedding light on the crime that rocked the Chattanooga Choo Choo right off its tracks."

She ended with a prayer for comfort for all the families hurting over the sudden loss of a loved one at the hands of brutality. Then she paused for a count of twenty to allow enough time for the rolling credits she would layer into the video during the editing process and pressed the stop button on the video app on the tablet she used for recording. She'd long since given up doing live videos, wishing to avoid reading any negative comments while on the air. Leaning back, she inhaled deeply and then exhaled slowly. After every podcast-recording session, it took her a few moments to steady her heart rate and calm the nervous anxiety. Three years as a true crime podcaster, and it still never got easier to discuss the gruesome details of the numerous murders that had taken place in her beautiful state of Tennessee.

"Lord, please give me strength to keep going with this work. I pray my podcast continues to shine a light on the darkness in this world as I seek justice for my beautiful Becca and for other families who have lost loved ones." She lifted her head and looked at the photo collage that decorated the opposite wall. Photos of her daughter. A smattering of baby photos, school photos and vacation photos, but the ones that tugged at her heart the most were the ones taken in the last months of Becca's life.

Becca holding her acceptance letter to Vanderbilt University in Nashville. Smiling in her senior portrait. Posing with her best friends at a school assembly. Sitting on a bunk bed in her cabin at church camp. And the last photo they'd taken together, one month before Becca died. Mother and daughter standing on the glass-bottomed section at the highest point on the SkyBridge in Gatlinburg, Becca laughing at her mother for holding on to the handrail so tightly her knuckles had turned white, fear plainly written on Jenna's face.

"Don't be so afraid to live, Mom," Becca had said, laughing. Seventeen and fearless. "We only get one life, embrace it. Be adventurous. Don't let fear hold you back."

As a constant reminder of her daughter's philosophy, Jenna had intertwined the photos with the words *Embrace life with an adventurous spirit. Don't allow fear to control you.*

"Oh, Becca, I wish you were here to see me now. I may not have gained an adventurous spirt, but I have definitely stepped way outside my comfort zone," she said aloud to the empty room. Who would have ever thought an introvert like Jenna would become the host of a podcast with half a million followers?

With a sigh, she pushed back her chair and stood. Jenna had skipped dinner, and it was nearing nine o'clock. If she hoped to watch the video she'd just recorded and make notes for edits and still be in bed before midnight, she needed to grab a cup of coffee and maybe a slice of the lemon pound cake she'd baked last night.

Leaving the lights off, she plodded down the hall toward the front of the house where the range-hood light shone like a beacon. As she neared the end of the hall, the large picture window in the living room exploded. Jenna gasped and dropped to a squatted position, wrapping both arms over her head. A thousand tiny fragments of glass rained down, and a large flat block dropped onto the center of the hardwood floor.

Not again. Her podcast anti-fans had gotten out of control, especially in the last two weeks. Someone had slashed her tires. The words *Let Becca R.I.P. or Join Her* had been spray-painted on her garage door. Then she'd found a photo—her head transposed onto a person's body in a coffin. It had been taped to her truck window in the grocery store parking lot.

Now this. Of course, she was used to these things by now. And when people tried scare tactics, it usually meant she was getting close to a breakthrough in one of the cold cases she featured on her podcast.

Oh, how she missed the days of living in a gated community. Things like this would have been less likely to happen if she still lived there. Unfortunately, when her ex-husband, Patrick, had left her for his secretary, Jenna had made the difficult decision to move her and five-year-old Becca back to Barton Creek, leaving Nashville and her cheating ex in the rearview mirror.

It had been hard to uproot her child and move her away from the only home she'd ever known and her friends and classmates, but Jenna had known living closer to family would be for the best. Her mom had provided free childcare, which allowed Jenna the opportunity to finish her degree in education. After graduation, she'd taught high school math while working on her masters in counseling. Then she had accepted the counselor position when it came available. Working in education had given her a schedule that allowed her to attend all Becca's school and sporting events.

She had no regrets over the sacrifices she'd made to give her only child the best upbringing she could, and she would cherish every memory. But if she let her mind wander, she sometimes wondered if Becca would still be alive if they'd stayed in Nashville. While there were no guarantees in life, if they hadn't been in Barton Creek, Becca wouldn't have been near the hiking trail where they'd discovered her body.

Saying goodbye to her beautiful, outgoing seventeen-year-old daughter had been the hardest moment of her life. But that pain had only intensified from not knowing whom Becca had been on the hiking trail with and why they'd killed her, leaving her body to be discovered by thru-hikers on the Appalachian Trail the next morning.

She pushed to her feet. Thankfully, she'd left her running shoes on instead of kicking them off halfway through the podcast like normal. Food would have to wait until she boarded up the window. It was a good thing she'd stocked up on plywood at the building-supply store the last time this had happened three weeks ago. She'd long given up the notion that she needed to report every little incident that occurred. The sheriff's department always did the best they could, but it was a waste of their time for her to keep filing reports when there wasn't any way to prove who had thrown the rock. And really, she doubted it was the same person committing each offense.

People had strong feelings about true crime podcasts, with some cheering her on in her efforts to uncover clues and assist the police in finding murderers, while others criticized her and accused her of planting evidence to fit her theories. It didn't matter that she gathered most of her information from public records and never visited a crime scene until the police had completed their investigation and removed all crime scene tape.

Not wanting her movements to be seen by anyone lingering outside, she left the lights off. Although she doubted the person who'd thrown the rock had stuck around. In her experience, the people who did this type of thing were more about making her life miserable, costing her money and shutting her up—figuratively, not literally—and would never hang around long enough to be identified. Navigating around furniture in the dark, Jenna made her way to the kitchen. Opening the door that led into the garage, she snaked out a hand and flipped on the light. Then she stepped into the small single-vehicle space, thankful there were no windows.

When vandals had first started attacking her home two and a half years ago, she'd set up a mini workshop inside the garage, which was why she parked her Chevrolet Colorado outside. Jenna sighed. After someone vandalized her truck last week, she'd had no choice but to order a utility shed to convert into a workshop. The contractor planned to pour the concrete pad next week, weather permitting, and then they could assemble the shed. The hit her savings account had taken was enormous, but she was afraid if she didn't get her truck back into the garage, the vandals would do more than slash a few tires. And she couldn't afford a new vehicle.

The picture window was eight feet wide and five feet tall, meaning that one sheet of four-by-eight plywood wouldn't be enough to cover the opening. She could split the difference and leave a six-inch gap at the top and bottom, but that would allow all kinds of creepy-crawly critters to come inside. Walking over to the stack of plywood leaned against the garage wall, she hefted one of the two sheets onto the sawhorses. Then she opened the metal cabinet and pulled out her goggles and the circular saw she had bought for herself for Mother's Day almost two years ago. Being a mother and no longer having her child here with her made the holiday extra hard. Typically, she would pick up a salad from a drive-through restaurant and have a picnic beside Becca's grave, giving her daughter a life update.

On that particular morning, she'd awoken to the sound of breaking glass—the first incident of a rock being thrown into her home. The police were called but couldn't do much, since no one saw who threw the rock. After phoning a local handyman and being told it would be a week before he'd be able to get to her house and do the repair, she'd driven herself to the home-improvement store and purchased all she needed to board up her window until the repairman could order and install a new one. When she finally made it to Becca's grave for her picnic, she talked about the supplies she'd purchased at the home-improvement store and laughed that she'd bought herself a saw for Mother's Day. She pictured Becca smiling and saying she would have bought her the exact same gift if she'd been there to celebrate.

Jenna ripped the plywood to the size she needed. She picked up the pink tool belt her sister, Amber, had given her last Christmas and fastened it around her waist, then looped an arm through the ladder so it rested on her left shoulder before she headed out the side door into the yard.

Pausing, she listened. All was quiet. Her nearest neighbor, a retired detective from Atlanta, lived three-tenths of a mile away. Glancing toward his house, she saw a light shining through the trees. If he hadn't made it perfectly clear when he'd moved in six months earlier what he thought of her "little podcast," she might have called him and asked for his help boarding up the window.

She rounded the side of the house and leaned the plywood and ladder against the brick wall. Thankfully, a flower box ran the length of the window, so the plywood could rest on it as she secured each side into place. A shiver ran up the length of her spine. The tiny hairs at the nape of her neck stood at attention. Someone was watching her. Bending as if she were picking something up off the ground, she peeked under her arm, searching. A bright moon overhead illuminated the front yard, but the woods on either side of her driveway were full of shadows, making it impossible to detect an intruder.

The sound of a vehicle penetrated the silence of the night, and she stood and turned toward it. An SUV came around the curve in the road, and the headlights flashed on a figure at the edge of the yard. She gasped and dashed through the garage and raced into the house, slamming the door behind her and bolting it.

Her phone. She needed to retrieve it from her studio and call 911. This meant running past the shattered living room window. Puffing out a breath, she ran as if the imagined boogeyman from her childhood had come to life and was chasing her. Only this wasn't imagined. A real person with evil intent lurked outside her home.

As she drew even with the picture window, a fiery flame hurtled toward her. A scream ripped from her throat, and she dove behind the couch. A Molotov cocktail hit the watercolor painting of a sunflower, which Becca had painted in eleventh grade, that hung on the wall to her left.

A second flaming bottle of liquid shattered against the hearth of the rock fireplace, and the rug burst into flames, quickly blocking her path to safety. The accelerant used in the Molotov cocktails did its intended job. Smoke filled the room. Her eyes watered and her lungs burned. She had to find a way out of the inferno. And fast. Or the police would have another murder to solve when they discovered her charred, dead body.

Sean Quinn pressed hard on the brakes and sharply turned his steering wheel to the left. Fire and smoke plumed out of Jenna's house. Taking the turn into his neighbor's driveway too fast, his SUV's back tires fishtailed on the gravel drive. He eased off the gas and regained control, then pressed the call button on his steering wheel and gave the command to dial 911.

Slamming on his brakes and coming to a stop in front of the garage, he quickly filled the emergency dispatcher in on the situation and rattled off the address. Then he jumped out of his vehicle and ran toward the front door. Someone had shattered the large picture window, and a couple of pieces of plywood were lying on the ground. A vandal had obviously started the fire. Did the plywood mean Jenna Hartley was outside and not in the house? Flames crawled up the curtains and shot toward the roof, making a hissing noise.

Where was she? He scanned the area. No sign of her. "Ms. Hartley... Jenna! Where are you?"

"Sean? Help!" A faint cry came from inside, followed by a fit of coughing. "I'm trapped."

"Okay. I'm coming." He sprinted up the porch steps and twisted the doorknob. Locked. The handle was warm but not scorching, which meant the fire hadn't spread too far into the entryway. Yet. He turned sideways and rammed his shoulder against the door. It didn't budge. *This will never work.*

Sean took a deep breath and released it slowly. *Think. There has to be another way in.*

He'd only been inside the house twice—once for coffee shortly after he'd moved to the area and once to return mail that had accidentally been placed in his mailbox—but he vaguely remembered the door that led into the kitchen from the back deck had glass on the top half. Sean jumped off the porch, grabbed a large rock from the flower bed border and raced around the house. The doorknob was cool to the touch. The fire had not spread from the front of the house. He peered inside. The range-hood light cast an eerie glow over the kitchen, and smoke danced in the archway opening that led to the dining room. Gripping the rock tightly, he smashed the bottom left pane of glass, clearing the tiny shards as quickly as possible, and then stuck his arm through the opening, feeling around until his hand touched the doorknob. Click. He twisted the knob, and the door popped open an inch.

Pulling his arm out of the window, he pushed the door wide and darted inside. Smoke assaulted him immediately. His lungs burned. He snatched the dish towel that lay on the countertop near the sink, turned on the water and saturated the cloth, then covered his mouth and nose with it.

"P-p-please…hur-hurry," Jenna choked out in a raspy voice.

He darted through the cased opening to the dining room. The French doors that led into the living room stood open, but flames blocked the entrance. The lights were off. He willed his vision to adjust, but the haze of the smoke was working against him. "Where are you?"

A deep hacking cough answered him. "Here," she said. "On the floor. Against the wall. Between the sofa and the side table."

He mentally visualized the layout of the room. "Closest to the dining room or the entry hall?"

"Entry." Another scratchy cough. "The fire is on both sides of me. There were two Molotov cocktails thrown."

Two? Whoever did this had meant to cause the most damage possible. Hoping to get a better view of the living room, where the light from the fire might give him more insight into the situation, Sean moved to his right and immediately bumped into the dining table. Steadying himself, his hands came in contact with a tablecloth. He balled it up in his hands and pulled it off the table. A clattering sound followed, indicating that he'd knocked a vase or something off the table.

"What was that?" Jenna asked, fear evident in her voice.

"Not sure. But hang tight. I'm coming around to the entry."

He raced back to the kitchen sink. Turning on the water once again, he shoved the tablecloth into the sink, quickly soaking it. Guided only by the light over the range, he made his way through the adjoining family room and then stepped into the entry hall. Sirens pierced the night. Help was on the way, but he couldn't wait for them to get there. He had to get Jenna outside. Now. "I need you to talk. Don't stop until I reach you. Got it?"

"Okay. After you cross…the threshold…go about four feet…"

He draped the tablecloth over his head and shoulders and ran through the inferno. Heat engulfed him, and he broke out in a sweat.

"Turn right… I'm against the…wall…"

Sean fought to get his bearings. She sounded like she was to his left. Had he gotten turned around? "Keep talking!"

Silence.

The siren drew closer.

"Jenna! Talk to me!"

A series of coughs. He spun in the direction they came from, stretched his hand out and down in front of him, and walked forward. His hand came in contact with her silky hair. She jumped up and threw her arms around him.

"You found me," she whispered into his neck. "I was so afraid." Sobs racked her body.

"Shh, it's okay. I've got you." He wrapped his arm around her and pulled her under the wet tablecloth. "The fire hasn't reached the entry hall yet. So once we run through the doorway, we'll be on the other side of it. Okay?"

Her head, still pressed against his shoulder, bobbed in agreement.

With his arm clasping her tightly to him, he walked forward until he thought they were in line with the opening and turned to face it. "Okay. Run!"

They raced through the fiery wall and burst into the entry hall just as two firefighters broke through the front door. Jenna collapsed against Sean. He swept her up into his arms and raced past the firefighters into the cool night air. "I need a medic!"

Dear Lord, please let her be okay. Don't let me have been too late again.

TWO

Jenna jolted back to consciousness as an oxygen mask covered her mouth and nose. The sudden burst of air startled her, and she twisted her head, trying to free herself.

"Try to relax. You're going to be okay," a calm female voice asserted. "Thankfully, your handsome neighbor came along just in time to save you. Now, concentrate on taking slow, steady breaths while I get your vitals."

Jenna blinked rapidly, desperate to get her vision to clear.

"Hold on. I'll put some liquid tears into your eyes. I'm sure they're dry from the smoke."

Fingers firmly held her left eyelid open wide, and a drop of cool liquid splashed into it. Then the process was repeated with the right eye. "There now."

She blinked twice. A pretty blond nurse about ten years her junior met her gaze. "Is that better?"

Jenna nodded. "Yes. Thank you," she whispered.

"Try not to talk. Your throat will be sore for a while. Because you passed out, the medics intubated you in the ambulance on transport to the ER." The other woman smiled and slipped a blood pressure cuff over Jenna's upper arm. The cuff tightened as air was pumped into it, then slowly released.

Jenna closed her eyes and focused on her breathing as the woman finished getting all her vitals. The oxygen calmed her burning lungs, and she no longer felt the fight-or-flight sensation she'd felt when she first came to. "What...time..."

"Nearing one a.m. You've been asleep for a while." The nurse slipped the cuff off her arm, folded it and placed it on a cart. "The medics gave you a Schedule 2 sedative in your IV so you wouldn't fight the tube going down your windpipe. Dr. Branson said you must have needed the extra rest for it to knock you out the way it did. But on the plus side, you didn't have to be awake while they ran all the bloodwork and other tests in the ER."

Jenna looked around. This didn't look like an ER room. There was a small straight-backed chair, a recliner and a private bathroom.

"Oh, you're not in the ER now," the chatty nurse said, reading her thoughts. "Dr. Branson moved you into a room. You're on the sixth floor, close to the nurses' station. We'll monitor you overnight. Hopefully, you'll be released tomorrow. Just a precaution, since you inhaled so much smoke and passed out."

Jenna had never passed out before. She had also never been trapped in a burning house before, either. In her forty-three years, this was the closest she'd come to death. And though she'd always believed in God and had spent her youth attending church services in which the preacher talked about the glory of heaven, the thought of dying still terrified her. Maybe because she'd not only shut all her coworkers and friends out of her life four years ago when Becca died, but she'd also shut out God. She prayed at the end of every podcast and went through the motions of being a Christian, but she hadn't opened her Bible or put effort into strengthening her relationship with the Lord. After all, what was the point in going to church and worshiping Him if He hadn't cared enough to protect the person Jenna loved most in this world?

Yet He'd saved Jenna. The thought hit like a bolt of lightning. *Why, Lord? Why save me and not Becca? She had so much to live for. If she'd lived, she would have been in her final year of her bachelor's degree and getting ready to start med school in the fall.* Tears burned her eyes, begging for release, and she didn't have the strength to fight them. Turning her head away from the nurse, she allowed the torrent of tears to flow freely down her face.

"I'll let you rest now. Buzz if you need anything," the nurse said cheerfully over the sound of the squeaky wheel on the cart being pushed toward the door.

"How's the patient?" Sean's baritone voice boomed from the hallway.

He couldn't see her like this—weak and crying. She scrubbed her hands over her cheeks and turned to face him. He and the nurse were deep in whispered conversation. The nurse smiled up at him as she leaned against the cart. Were they discussing Jenna? Maybe she should clear her throat to get their attention.

"Ahem." The oxygen mask muffled her voice. She grasped the mask and pulled it down to her chin and tried again. *"Ahem."*

The force of clearing her throat sent her into a coughing fit. Two pairs of eyes turned in her direction. Her cheeks warmed. Well, the attempt to capture their attention subtly hadn't gone as planned.

"Ms. Hartley, you must leave the oxygen mask on."

The nurse grabbed a notepad off the cart, stuck it under her arm, and strode back to the bed and positioned the mask over Jenna's nose and mouth once again. Holding out the notepad, she added, "Here. Use this if you need to communicate. Okay?"

Fighting the urge to pull the covers over her head after being scolded in front of Sean, Jenna accepted the notepad with a sparkly pink pin clipped to the front and nodded, keeping her gaze turned to the floor.

"I'm sure Ms. Hartley knows how to follow directions." Sean's voice had a hint of laughter to it. She lifted her head and met his gaze. There was laughter shining in his cornflower blue eyes.

"Alrighty, then." The nurse gave Jenna one more glare before turning to Sean with a brilliant smile on her face. "Don't stay too long. Our patient needs her rest."

He returned her smile with one of his own, punctuated by dimples. "I promise—" he bent slightly to read her name tag "—Bethany. I'll only stay ten minutes."

"Okay. Make sure to stop by the desk and say goodbye on your way out." Bethany giggled and left the room.

Jenna stared after the young woman. What was she thinking, openly flirting with Sean like that? He had to be at least fifteen or sixteen years older than her—practically old enough to be her father.

"You don't have to look so shocked that a pretty woman would flirt with me." Sean pulled the straight-backed chair closer to the bed and dropped into the seat. "I may have gray at the temples, but I'm not ancient yet."

"You—" A burning sensation shot up her esophagus. She closed her eyes and swallowed.

"Use the notepad." He reached across and tapped the small pad in her hand.

She unhooked the pen and flipped open the cover. Then she scribbled. YOU'RE FLATTERED.

His chest shook as a deep chuckle filled the room. "Who wouldn't be? But being flattered by the attention is as far as it goes. I'm not interested. In her *or* a relationship. I enjoy my solitude. Now…" He leaned closer, searching her eyes. "How are you?"

I'M OKAY.

Sean cocked an eyebrow and waited.

REALLY.

"Good. Any idea who threw a Molotov cocktail into your home?"

She scribbled feverishly. NOT ONE. TWO!

Sean nodded. "Yes. The fire chief confirmed there were two. They're testing the accelerant and trying to lift fingerprints off of the broken bottles. But back to my question… Do you have any idea who would do such a thing?"

Didn't he think she would have already said something if she knew who had started the fire? Pressing her lips together, she shook her head. A sharp pain struck behind her left eye. She winced and rubbed her temple.

Sean was at her side in an instant. "Are you okay? Do you need me to call the nurse?"

"No," she replied, more sharply than she intended, and then winced at the sound of her raspy voice. She didn't like the way most medicines made her feel, often preferring not to take anything.

He tapped the notepad.

Making eye contact, she sighed and picked up the pen

and paper. I DON'T NEED THE NURSE. I'M FINE. JUST TIRED.

"Okay. I'll get going. Sheriff Dalton wants you to give a statement. I told him to wait until they release you from the hospital so that you can be well rested and clearheaded enough to give him details of what happened."

Heath Dalton complying with his request surprised her. She knew they were fishing buddies, but she hadn't realized they were close enough that Heath would take investigation advice from Sean. She'd known Heath his entire life. Their mothers had been close friends, and Jenna, being ten years older than Heath, had babysat him many times. One thing she learned early on was that Heath didn't like anyone telling him how to do things. That meant he must really respect her neighbor's opinion.

Sean picked up the notepad and wrote on it. "Here's my number. Call me if you need anything."

That's not going to happen. If Jenna needed something, she'd buzz the nurse. Or phone the police if it was something serious. Knowing if she shrugged or shook her head no he'd not leave until she recanted, and not wanting to lie by implying agreement, she looked at him silently.

Sean rubbed the back of his neck and gave a slight nod. "Get some rest." He turned on his heels and walked out of the room, closing the door behind him.

A shiver racked her body as an icy chill enveloped the room. Had she seemed ungrateful? Jenna lowered the head of her bed and sank under the covers. She would have to think of a way to apologize and thank him for saving her life. Maybe a red velvet cake. She giggled. Was that what her life was worth these days? A boxed cake mix and a small amount of time?

He probably didn't eat sweets, though she knew little about his eating habits—or anything else, for that matter. Only that he grew up in Atlanta but had visited his grandparents in Barton Creek every summer as a child. He'd inherited their farm when they passed away in an automobile accident two years ago. After retiring from the Atlanta PD, Sean had moved here to—in his words— "live a simpler life."

She had loved having his grandparents, Jim and Lois Ferguson, as neighbors and had tried to build a neighborly relationship with Sean when he arrived in Barton Creek six months ago. But the only thing he'd wanted was to tell her that her podcast was reckless and she needed to leave crime investigations to the police. *Like they'd done such an excellent job when Becca was murdered.*

Why did Sean have to be the one to save me? Now he'll have even more reason to believe he's right.

Jenna gasped and jerked awake. A dark shadow stood at the edge of her peripheral vision. She couldn't move, her body paralyzed. Soon, the sound of the monitors penetrated her consciousness. Frozen in fear, she forced herself to focus on her breathing. The shadow never moved. Gradually, her body relaxed, and the rhythm of her heart returned to normal. Logic settled over her like a warm blanket. She was in the hospital. Everything was okay. The shadow wasn't a bad guy in her room. This was an episode of sleep paralysis, like she had suffered from as an adolescent and again following Becca's death. Brought on by stress. Her imagination was in overdrive because of the trauma she'd been through. What time was it? She felt as if she'd barely fallen asleep, but the light peeking through the blinds proved it was morning.

Her hand brushed the call button. The nurse had said to buzz if she needed anything. Did that include having someone open the blinds so the sunlight would chase away imaginary shadows? Only one way to find out. She closed her hand around the call button.

A gruff male voice came from the shadow. "No one can save you."

Jenna gasped, and the call button remote slipped from her hand.

The shadow snickered. "I've been watching you sleep. I was afraid you wouldn't wake in time."

She frantically patted around the mattress. Where was the call button? The shadow charged forward, grabbed the cord attached to the button with a gloved hand and dangled it above her head. She reached for the device, and he slung it behind the headboard.

"I'm sorry," the man said in a mock-apologetic voice. "I can't allow you to call the nurse, because then I'd have to kill her, too. And I don't like killing innocent people."

Lifting a shaky hand to the oxygen mask, she pulled it away from her nose, then hesitated. If the mask were around her neck, it would be too easy for him to grasp it and strangle her. She snatched the mask over her head and shoved it behind her, her eyes never leaving the shadow figure.

The man wore dark jeans, a black turtleneck and a white lab coat. A surgical hat and mask covered his hair, nose and mouth. She itched to reach out and snatch the mask off his face but knew it would be a waste of energy. The man was tall, well above six feet. Even if he bent over slightly, she'd never grasp the mask.

"What—" She swallowed in a futile attempt to moisten her throat. "What do you want?"

The man's body quaked, and a soft chortle reached her ears. "I'm sure you know the answer to that question." He pulled a small vial out of his coat pocket and then quickly filled a syringe with the liquid. "After all the torment you've put me through, my only regret is this won't be the painful death I'd envisioned, but at least you woke up in time so I can watch the fear in your eyes." He plunged the needle into the access port midway up her IV line.

"No!" A burst of adrenaline surged through her. Jenna rolled to her left and flipped over the low bed rail, landing with a thud on the floor on the opposite side of the bed from the man. The intravenous catheter in her hand tugged painfully as the IV tubing stretched taut, blood dripping down her arm.

"Sorry, darlin', but that maneuver won't save you." He held up the empty needle, then dropped it onto the bed. "A high dose of Propofol is already working its way into your bloodstream."

"No, no, no," she muttered under her breath, and yanked the partially extracted IV line out.

He rounded the bed with a low, guttural growl. His body shook as he stretched his hands forward. If he got them around her neck, he'd choke the life out of her. She rolled under the bed, scooting as far as she could from the hands that reached for her. The door to her room creaked open a few inches and stopped. She locked eyes with her tormentor.

"Sean, I'm surprised to see you here so early," Nurse Bethany said cheerfully from the other side of the door.

Sean is here! Hope surged inside Jenna.

"I'm an early riser. Thought I'd come see how our patient is doing and hang around to give her a ride home
once she's discharged," Sean replied. "If you're headed
in to check vitals and things, I can stay out here until
you've finished."

"Looks like your neighbor saved you once more. You
won't be so fortunate a third time," her tormentor ground
out through clenched teeth. Then he straightened and
rounded the foot of the bed.

"Sean! Stop him!" Jenna yelled.

The door to the room flew open, and the shadow man
shoved the rolling bedside-tray table at the two people
standing in the doorway.

Sean pulled Bethany out of the way, and Shadow Man
darted past them.

"Check on Jenna. And call security," Sean ordered
as he pushed a small backpack into the stunned nurse's
hands. Then he sprinted after the man.

Jenna scooted out from under the bed, grabbed the
side rail and pulled herself to her feet, her knees shaking.

"Are you okay?" Bethany rushed to her, lowered the
bed rail and helped ease her onto the bed.

"Yes, just shaken."

"Your IV catheter came out. I'll get it replaced and then
reconnect it." Bethany snatched the call button remote.

"No!" Jenna puffed out a breath, grasped the top of the
discarded syringe with the tips of two fingers and held it
up. "He put Propofol in the IV."

A male orderly rolled the tray table back into the room.
"I called security. Is everything okay?"

"There was an attempt on Ms. Hartley's life. She's okay
but understandably shaky. I need to notify the on-call

doctor, let him know the attacker may have drugged her," Bethany replied.

"I don't think any got into my system." Jenna dropped the syringe onto the tray and leaned back against the pillow as she blinked rapidly, fighting to keep her eyes open. "The IV came loose when I tried to get away."

Bethany checked her vitals, then made eye contact with the orderly. "Stay with her." She patted Jenna's shoulder and rushed out of the room.

Jenna turned toward the window. A bright streak of light peeked around the sides of the window covering. "Could you please turn on the light and open the blinds?"

The orderly followed her instructions, and soon fluorescent light mixed with morning sunlight filled the room. The Appalachian Mountains stood proudly in the distance. Their snowcapped peaks were like a soothing balm to her soul. A yearning to hike the numerous trails the way she had many times as a single mother, praying and surrounding herself in God's beauty, washed over her.

Be strong and of a good courage; be not afraid, neither be thou dismayed: for the LORD thy God is with thee whithersoever thou goest. Joshua 1:9—the verse she'd comforted herself with after Patrick had run off with his secretary—echoed in her mind. She'd clung to that verse as a single mom in her midtwenties. But she hadn't given it much thought these last four years. Was God still with her even after all this time?

"Rest, Ms. Hartley, and let us take care of you."

The orderly's words pulled her from her thoughts. Jenna narrowed her eyes at him. He had been quick to show up. Could the orderly be Shadow Man? No. He wasn't tall enough, and his build was too lanky. Besides, he wore light blue scrubs with a long-sleeved white T-shirt underneath his top. He couldn't have changed clothes that quickly.

Her vision blurred, and she felt faint. *No.* Had the drugs reached her bloodstream after all? *Resist the urge. Stay awake. Focus on the sunlight.*

THREE

Sean stepped into the elevator and jabbed the button for the sixth floor. The hospital was eerily silent this time of morning. He scrubbed his hand over his face, then pressed the Door Close button. What was taking the elevator doors so long to close? He pressed the button twice more. Just as they started to close, a hand reached inside and halted them.

The large metal doors opened once more, and a tall gentleman in his early sixties, wearing a suit and tie, stepped into the elevator and pressed the button for the top floor. "Most people don't realize pressing the Door Close button doesn't really speed things up. Because of the Americans with Disabilities Act, federal law requires that the doors stay open long enough for those with crutches or a wheelchair to get in the elevator."

"Then why haven't they removed the button?"

The white-haired man stepped back and made eye contact. "I've asked that same question myself many times." He held out his hand. "Jefferson Price, CEO of Knoxville General Hospital."

Sean accepted the handshake. "Sean Quinn. Nice to meet you."

"Well, Mr. Quinn, what brings you to our fine hospital so early in the morning?"

Sean narrowed his eyes. Could this man be Jenna's attacker? He was the right height and build. No. The man he'd chased wouldn't have had time to change and would surely be out of breath. "I'm visiting a friend."

"Your face is red and sweaty, as if you ran to get here. Is everything okay? You didn't receive bad news, did you? If you'd like, I can have the hospital chaplain visit your friend."

Having spent his entire life in the southern United States, Sean knew some people in the south tended to be overly friendly, but this man's chattiness seemed excessive, especially this early in the morning.

"Everything is fine," he replied, never one to share more information than needed.

Mr. Price reached into his inner coat pocket and pulled out a business card. "Well, if you need anything, or even if you want to file a complaint about the slow elevators, don't hesitate to reach out to my office."

The elevator stopped, and the doors opened. They'd reached the sixth floor. Accepting the business card, Sean stepped out of the elevator without looking back. Even if he liked the practice of small talk, there was no time to engage in it at the moment. He'd chased Jenna's dark-clad assailant down the stairs, losing him somewhere between the second and fourth floors. Now he needed to check on Jenna and make sure she was okay.

The nurses' station was vacant. He glanced at his watch. 7:23 a.m. Shift change typically occurred in most hospitals at seven o'clock—at least according to his sister Marilee, who was an ICU nurse. Maybe the day shift nurses were making their morning rounds. He made his way down the hall to Jenna's room, pushed open the door and froze. Bethany, another nurse and a doctor surrounded Jenna's bed.

He rushed to the unoccupied spot at the foot of the bed. Jenna's eyes were closed, her dark hair splayed across her pillow, framing her pale heart-shaped face. He couldn't tell if she was breathing or not. "Is she okay?" he asked hesitantly.

"Who are you?" The doctor, who had shoulder-length brown hair and looked like he was barely out of high school, looked up, noticing Sean for the first time.

"Oh, he's Ms. Hartley's hero. He's saved her twice— first when he pulled her from the fire and again when he stopped the attack this morning." Bethany smiled and turned to Sean. "We need a few more minutes. Could you wait in the hall?"

He hesitated, unable to make his feet move. Why was he so worried about a neighbor he'd only spoken to a handful of times? It couldn't be because he'd saved her life. He'd saved many lives during his time with the Atlanta PD and had never felt a sense of responsibility like the one that kept him glued to the floor in this hospital room.

"Please." The doctor swept his hand toward the door. "I'll be out in a minute to talk to you."

Sean cast one last glance at Jenna, praying he'd see her chest move or hear a snore—anything. Nothing. He shuffled toward the door. She had to be alive. If she weren't, the hospital staff wouldn't just be standing around. Would they? *Wait!* He pivoted on one foot and craned his neck to look at the vitals monitor mounted on top of a pole with wheels that sat beside the head of the bed. A jagged heartbeat line meandered across the top of the screen.

Heart rate: 53 bpm. Blood pressure: 117/69. He released the breath he'd been holding since entering the room. She was alive.

"Sean. Go. Now." Bethany gave him a pointed look, and he turned and slipped out of the room.

A young male orderly and a security guard walked over to him.

"You're the one who chased after the man who tried to hurt Ms. Hartley, aren't you?" the orderly questioned.

"Yes, but I didn't catch him."

"Could you identify the guy?" the security guard asked.

"No. I wasn't able to get close enough." Sean scanned the ceilings and pointed at a camera. "Can't you zoom in on the security tapes and get a close-up of him?"

"We'll try, but I'm not holding out much hope. One of my guys caught a glimpse of the man as he raced out of the building. Said he wore a covering over his head and face."

"Yeah, that's what I thought, too." Sean shoved his hand through his hair, as had become his habit since letting it grow out after he retired from the police force. "I hope they release Jenna today, but if they don't, could you station a guard outside her door? This is the second attempt on her life."

"We don't normally offer private security, but I'll talk to my boss and see what we can arrange. If she has to stay overnight again."

Sean leaned in and read the guard's name tag. "Thanks, Aaron. I really appreciate it."

Bethany exited the room with the other nurse. "She's going to be fine." She placed a hand on Sean's shoulder. "Dr. Davidson will give you a full update." She motioned for the orderly to follow her to the nurses' station.

The doctor stepped into the hall and pulled the door closed behind him. Sean walked over to him and held out his hand. "Dr. Davidson, I'm Sean Quinn. Ms. Hartley is my—" How should he identify himself? If he said *neighbor*, the doctor might not give him any information. He could say *friend*, but that was a bit of a stretch and carried little weight for getting personal information on someone in the hospital.

"I know who you are, Mr. Quinn. Bethany has made it clear that you are a knight in shining armor." The doctor grinned.

Sean shrugged. "More like a neighbor who was in the right place at the right time."

"Well, that's a good thing for Ms. Hartley." A solemn expression replaced the doctor's smile. "In all seriousness, Ms. Hartley will be okay. But the man who attacked her tried to give her an overdose of Propofol. Thankfully, she managed to pull her IV catheter out so only a small amount actually reached her bloodstream."

"Is that why she's sleeping?" Sean probed.

"Yes. But she's already starting to come back around, and her vitals are strong. We'll watch her a few hours. Then she should be able to go home this afternoon." The doctor turned and crossed to the nurses' station, effectively cutting off any further questions.

Sean met the guard's gaze. "I'll stay with Ms. Hartley until she's released, so no need to worry about posting someone outside her door. But a police report should be filed."

"Yes, sir. We'll take care of that on our end." The guard hurried down the hall.

Sean entered Jenna's room. She stared at him, and her

lower lip trembled. Though their interactions had been minimal over the last six months—primarily because he'd opened his big mouth about the dangers of her playing amateur detective—she had never struck him as a woman who was afraid of anything. Fierce. Determined. Justice fighter. Independent. Loyal. Those were the words that described his neighbor. Of course, two attempts on her life in nine hours would justify fear. He could only hope she'd take these attacks seriously, shut down her podcast and let the police handle things from here on out. If not, he'd have to step in and help protect her because there was no way the sheriff's department had a large enough force to assign someone to guard her.

Jenna climbed into Sean's SUV, closed the door and dropped the bag with her smoke-infused clothes onto the floorboard. Then she clicked her seat belt into place as Sean settled into the driver's seat. She folded her hands in her lap and looked down at the extra-large Atlanta Braves sweatshirt and gray sweatpants with the drawstring waist pulled as tight as it could go. "Thank you for bringing me a change of clothes."

"You're welcome." He backed out of the parking space. "I'm sorry they're too big."

"It's okay. They're warm and don't smell of smoke. That's all that matters."

Silence blanketed the vehicle.

Jenna hated chitchat, but the idea of spending the forty-minute drive in awkward silence was worse. "I'm sorry you were stuck at the hospital all day, waiting to drive me home. I could have called a rideshare service."

"It was important to have someone standing guard over you. What if the guy who attacked you came back?"

The question was rhetorical, so she didn't bother to reply. They both knew perfectly well that if the guy had shown up again, she might not have survived.

He paid to exit the parking garage and merged into traffic. "So, what's the plan?"

"What do you mean?"

"Where are you going to live while your home is re-built? They contained the fire in the living room, but the damage was extensive. You can't stay there. Do you have a safe place you can go? Somewhere the person after you won't know to look?"

"I haven't really given that any thought." She furrowed her brow. "But I'll figure something out. Just drop me off at home. I'll pack some clothes, grab my laptop and book a room somewhere."

"I know we've not really seen eye to eye on things since I moved here." He pulled to a stop at a red light, turned to her and frowned. "I overstepped. It wasn't my place to tell you to stop your podcast. But my concerns were—" A horn honked behind them, and he turned his focus back to the road.

"Look, I don't want to hear *I told you so*, okay? Unless you've lost someone you love in such a senseless manner, you have no right to judge me."

"Actually, I have. My wife," Sean mumbled. "And I wasn't trying to judge you or your motives. I understood them perfectly. However, I know all too well how civilians with good intentions sometimes hinder an investigation while putting themselves in danger and creating more work for the law enforcement officers involved in the case."

Jenna digested his words and swallowed her anger. She'd known he was a widower, but she'd never heard how his wife had died. A thousand questions raced through her mind. It wasn't her place to ask about his pain. In different circumstances, they might have been able to discuss their losses and maybe even be friends, but she doubted that would ever be possible now. She'd put up too many defensive walls when he'd first moved in and she'd felt judged by every word out of his mouth. It didn't help that he was right.

She *had* created more work for the police department. In the beginning, she'd called them to her house every time someone vandalized her property. She probably made twenty calls to the sheriff's office in three months before realizing the vandals were too smart to get caught. Even installing a video doorbell and cameras outside her home hadn't helped. The vandals always seemed to attack late at night and stayed in the shadows, not offering any identifying clues.

"I'm sorry. I should have realized you spoke from experience." She examined his profile. "Was your wife's murderer caught?"

The vein in his neck twitched. "Yes. Ten months after she…passed."

"I'm glad they solved her case before it became cold." She turned back around in her seat and faced forward. The first few months after Becca was gone, Jenna had held on to so much hope that the police would find the person responsible for her murder. With each passing month, she'd become less hopeful. On the one-year anniversary of her child's death, Jenna had recorded her first podcast. Six months later, she'd walked away from her position as the high school counselor to be a full-time podcaster, desperate to help the police find the clues necessary to solve the case before it hit the three-year mark. The point where, according to the former sheriff Matt Rice, unsolved cases officially became cold cases.

They rode in silence. Forty minutes later, they reached Barton Creek. With a population of twenty-five hundred, Jenna knew how blessed their town was to be untouched by the droves of tourists who flocked to the region yearly, visiting the Great Smoky Mountains National Park and nearby Gatlinburg and Pigeon Forge.

She'd always loved her hometown, situated in the foothills of the Appalachian Mountains. Which was why, after Patrick had left her, she'd moved back with her young child in tow. She had wanted her daughter to grow up in a small town where everyone looked out for one another—which made Becca's unsolved murder all the more torturous.

"We're here," Sean announced, pulling her from her thoughts. "I spoke with the fire chief this morning. He said to caution you to stay out of the room with the damage because he's not sure how structurally sound the roof is on that section of the house and doesn't want it caving in with you inside."

Sean activated his blinker, turned into her driveway and parked. Jenna gasped. She had known there had been a lot of fire and smoke but hadn't been prepared to see the busted-out picture window and soot-stained brick. Exiting the vehicle, she crinkled her nose at the smoldering stench and stared open-mouthed at the damage in front of her.

Tears burned the backs of her eyes, but she blinked them away. She would not wallow in grief. Her home could be replaced. However, she wouldn't stop until she found the person responsible. The attack could only mean she was finally getting close to finding her daughter's murderer.

Sean came to stand beside her. "Are you okay?"

She nodded and turned at the sound of a vehicle door closing. Sheriff Heath Dalton walked toward them, concern etched on his face. "Jenna, are you okay?"

"I'm fine, Heath." She offered a forced smile. "I'm sure you're a busy person. You didn't need to drive out here to get my statement. I could have given it to one of your deputies."

"But then I wouldn't have an excuse to check on you and make sure you're truly okay." He searched her face. Seemingly satisfied that she was holding up under the pressure of the attacks, he turned to Sean and clapped him on the back. "How are you doing? I got a call from Knoxville Police Chief Dan Graves. He wanted to fill me in on the incident at the hospital."

"Gotta love small towns and how fast news travels." Sean smiled. "In Atlanta, it could take days to know about related incidences. Usually, there were so many eyewitness accounts and different takes that the actual details of the crime would get complicated."

Jenna examined her neighbor with fresh eyes. She'd spent many an evening sitting on Jim and Lois Ferguson's porch, listening to them speak of their grandson, the big-city detective. Lois had always looked forward to the weekly phone calls with him. While Jenna had known he was a retired detective, she'd never really thought about what pushed him to dissuade her from continuing her podcast. This explained why he'd been so vocal.

"I also heard you risked your life to save Jenna last night when you didn't wait for the fire department to get here."

"Just doing the neighborly thing." Sean pinned her with his gaze. "I may have grown up in a bustling city, but my parents taught me to care about what happens in my community and to look out for my neighbors."

She fought the urge to squirm under his scrutiny. A chill washed over her, and she rubbed her arms. "If you guys will excuse me. I'll go pack some things and then see if I can find a place to stay for the next few weeks."

"Do you—"

"Let me—"

"No. I don't need either of you coming into my home with me. I am capable of packing my own bags." Sean opened his mouth to speak, and she rushed on. "I promise I won't go into the living room. You've already told me it's dangerous."

"Okay, then."

Heath turned to Sean. "I brought a couple of tarps and a ladder. If you'll give me a hand, we should be able to get the damaged area of the house covered by the time she's finished packing."

"There's a ladder and plywood—" Jenna looked at the front of the house where she'd placed the items last night. "Never mind. Looks like they were damaged in the fire."

"Don't worry about it. We'll get it covered well enough that it's weather proofed," Sean told her.

"Okay. And, since I know you'll both offer, while I'm packing you can decide who'll escort me to my temporary

home. But just know, whoever is tasked with that responsibility is only following me to make sure I make it there
safely and will not stick around afterward as a guard.
I'm an adult woman. And I refuse to have a babysitter."

She turned and made her way into the house as the
men talked in hushed tones behind her. Before long, she
had packed a small suitcase with clothes that needed to
be washed the minute she reached the place she would be
staying. They may have contained the fire to the living
room, but the smell of smoke had penetrated the entire
house and all its contents.

Jenna crossed the hall and entered the room she used
as a studio. Opening the closet, she knelt and opened her
fireproof safe and removed the documents pertaining to
Becca's case that she'd collected over the years. She pulled
a backpack off the top shelf and placed the documents,
her laptop and recording equipment into it. Then she went
over to the wall of photos and removed the one of her and
Becca on the SkyBridge and placed it in the front zippered
section of the backpack.

One more thing to do. She picked up her phone and
bit her lip. Should she call Amber? No. Her sister would
insist she come to Nashville to stay with her, but Jenna
needed to be in Barton Creek to oversee the repairs of her
home. And to continue to untangle the clues to Becca's
murder. Maybe Jenna could book a room at the Hideaway
Inn Bed and Breakfast, run by her mother's best friend
Frances Nolan. No. Jenna couldn't risk leading danger
to Ms. Frances.

She could go stay at her parents' house in Maryville
until they returned from their Caribbean cruise. Only, if
she did that, they'd want her to stay with them until the

repairs to her home had been completed. And she couldn't put them at risk any more than she could her sister or Ms. Frances. She puffed out a breath. It might be easier to hide in a tourist area. She'd drive to Gatlinburg and find a hotel with a room she could rent for an extended stay.

Okay, time to go.

She slipped her arms through the backpack's straps and returned to her bedroom. Picking up her purse off the dresser, she dug inside for her keys so she could start her vehicle remotely and allow it a few moments to warm up. For whatever reason, she couldn't seem to shake the chill that had descended on her earlier. The February temperatures could be to blame. But she suspected it was more nerves than anything, as the cold had never bothered her before.

Jenna snagged her down jacket off the hanger on the back of her bedroom door and then made her way to the front of the house. When she stepped onto the front porch, she was amazed to discover that the men had finished their task and were standing beside the sheriff's truck, engaged in conversation.

"Hold on, I'll get your bags!" Sean yelled, and headed across the yard in her direction.

Heath lifted a hand in farewell, settled into his vehicle and started backing down the drive. As Sean climbed the porch steps, Jenna pointed her key fob at her truck and pushed the remote start button. The parking lights flashed, and the engine sprang to life.

A loud explosion, followed by a bright flash of light and a rush of hot air, shook the world around her. Glass and metal rained down on the lawn. Sean dove toward her and pushed her through the open front door. They landed in a tangled heap on the hardwood floor of her foyer.

"Are you okay?" he asked huskily in her ear.

Jenna nodded, unable to form words. Someone had planted a bomb in her truck. *Dear Lord, how many more times can I escape death?*

Whatever it took, she had to stay alive long enough to see Becca's murderer brought to justice.

FOUR

Sean grasped the doorframe and drug himself to his feet, then reached out his hand to Jenna. She slipped her hand into his, and he pulled her upward until they stood face-to-face.

"Are you sure you're not injured?" He looked her up and down. Other than a scratch on her face, she seemed unharmed. This time.

"I'm fine." She pushed past him and stepped through the open doorway. "Unfortunately, my truck isn't."

"A vehicle is replaceable. People are not." He picked up her jacket, which had fallen onto the porch, shook it out and draped it around her shoulders. Her body was shaking. Sean rubbed his hands over her shoulders. It would be easy for her to slip into a state of shock, given all that she'd been through. "Why did you use the remote start?"

"Habit, I guess." She shrugged one shoulder. "I always use it during the winter months so the seats warm up before I get inside."

"Are you both okay?" Heath jogged toward them. He'd parked his cruiser at the edge of the road, blue lights flashing. "Do we need an ambulance?"

"There are no obvious physical injuries. But it wouldn't hurt to have a medic come check out Jenna."

"No." She shook her head, frowning at him. "I'm fine."

Their gazes locked, and he searched her chocolate-colored eyes. When she refused to look away, he pressed his lips together and dipped his head.

"Yes or no?" Heath stood a few feet from the porch, staring up at them.

"No ambulance, just the fire department," Sean replied. "They're already en route."

Turning to look at Jenna's truck—the cab fully engulfed in flames—Sean gasped. "My vehicle! I've gotta move it!"

He jumped off the small porch and raced to his SUV, which sat a few feet behind Jenna's truck. Intense heat assailed him as he drew near. His windshield had a large crack, and the paint on the hood had bubbled. Slipping his hand into his denim jacket, he used it as a makeshift oven mitt to allow him to touch the hot door handle. Then he hopped into the driver's seat, turned the key he'd left dangling in the ignition and, without even shutting his door, quickly backed away from the flames. The sound of sirens rang out as he parked his SUV, close to the sheriff's cruiser.

Jenna and Heath made their way across the lawn to a large oak tree, her luggage in tow. Sean jogged over to them as the first fire truck pulled into the driveway.

"Is your vehicle damaged?" Jenna asked, her eyes wide.

The concern etched on her face made his knees buckle. His wife, Felicia, had had a similar expression on her face when she'd been shot outside their home. Sean had witnessed the shooting, and he'd dropped to his knees beside the woman he'd loved for two decades and yelled for the next-door neighbor who'd ventured outside to call 911. Then he'd held his wife's head in his lap and pressed his hands against her chest, desperate to stop the flow of blood.

"Sean... Sean!" Jenna's concerned voice sounded miles away.

Heath placed a hand on his shoulder. "Are you okay, buddy?"

Shaking his head, Sean pulled himself back to the present. "Sorry." He closed his eyes and counted to three before meeting Jenna's gaze. "Don't worry about my vehicle. The damage is minor. It's drivable."

He turned to Heath. "Does she need to stay here for this, or can I take her to my place?"

"No, I need—"

"Actually, Jenna," Heath said, interrupting whatever she had been about to say, "Sean's right. It would be a good idea for you to wait at his house. There's nothing you can do here."

Jenna looked over her shoulder. "The blue tarp you put up has melted. I need to board up my house."

Heath grasped her shoulders and turned her to face him. "I'm not going anywhere until the fire is out and the vehicle has been transported to the impound lot so the forensic team can go over it. While I'm waiting, I'll call someone to come out and board up the window with plywood. And, before I leave, I'll lock up the house."

"Okay." Jenna's shoulders slumped. "I hate to ask, after you've done so much, but I thought I'd get a hotel room in Gatlinburg for the night. Could you maybe drive me there later?"

Heath frowned. "I don't think that's a good idea. You need to be somewhere we can protect you."

She placed a hand on her hip. "Does that mean you're going to assign an officer to guard me?"

Heath scratched his head. "I'll figure something out. Just wait at Sean's until I'm finished here."

"I'll protect her," Sean interjected. Now, why had he said that? He'd warned Jenna her podcast would make extra work for the sheriff's office, but there was no way Heath had the personnel to assign a guard to watch Jenna around the clock. Sean puffed out a breath and met two pairs of eyes. "You don't have the man power, Heath, and it's not like I'm a novice trying to play cops and robbers."

"Both are valid points," Heath acknowledged, turning to Jenna. "I think it's the best plan."

"I can't stay in a home—alone—with a man. The neighbors will talk."

Sean bit back a retort that her virtue was safe with him. He'd been married to the love of his life; they'd had a beautiful nineteen years together. He wasn't looking to replace Felicia. Being a widowed hermit suited him just fine.

But of course, he also knew she was right. No matter how honorable his intentions were, people liked to talk, especially in a small town. "Look, we don't have a lot of options here. Unless you want to hire a private security firm. I've heard good things about the Protective Instincts office in Knoxville." He raised an eyebrow, and she turned to survey her damaged home and vehicle.

He felt like a heel for pushing her like this, but she had to realize she wouldn't be safe on her own. "You can stay in the house. I'll bunk in my camper."

"Will you be able to hear her from the camper if someone breaks into the house?" Heath queried.

"I'm a light sleeper. Besides, I'll leave Beau in the house with her. He'll wake me."

"Beau?" Jenna cocked her head.

The fire chief ambled over to them. "Sheriff, my men have extinguished the flames, but I'll have a couple of guys stick around for a little while to make sure the fire doesn't reignite."

"I appreciate that, Fred. I'll call the tow truck. Should take them about thirty minutes to get here," Heath replied.

"I'll let the boys know." Fred tipped his head at Jenna. "Ma'am." Then he turned and walked away.

Once the chief was out of earshot, Heath turned his focus back to Jenna. "I can't force you to stay with Sean. But I need you to understand—if you don't take him up on his generous offer, you're being reckless and you could put innocent lives in danger. Whoever is after you is getting more brazen. And the best way for you to stay alive is to let Sean protect you."

She wet her lips and swallowed. Sean hated for anyone to live in fear, but he understood Heath's need to make her realize the seriousness of the situation.

After several long minutes, Jenna nodded. "Okay. Thank you, Sean. I'll accept your offer. And I appreciate it."

Heath hugged Jenna. "Wise decision. Now, get some rest." *Even if it means giving up my warm bed and sleeping in my camper on a cold winter's night.* Felicia would have expected him to help a neighbor in distress, and even if she was no longer around to witness his actions, he still wanted to live his life in a manner that would make her proud. Not only that, but if he could help capture the guy who was after Jenna and solve her daughter's murder, maybe she'd give up her podcast and things would become a little more peaceful around here. *Yeah, keep telling yourself that, man. Don't admit—even to yourself—that you're not doing this for the peace but because protecting innocent people and solving murders is in your blood. You may be retired, but you miss the action and the adrenaline rush.*

Jenna added a scoop of detergent to the washing machine, closed the lid and pressed the start button. "Thanks for letting me do a load of laundry." She crossed into the kitchen, where Sean stood at the stove, preparing omelets. "It surprised me that my clothes smelled so strongly of smoke, since the fire was contained in the living room."

"It happens." He smiled and motioned toward the table. "Have a seat. Your supper is ready."

"You didn't have to prepare me a meal. I can cook for myself." She slipped into a chair at the round table in the breakfast nook.

"I know. But since you don't know your way around my kitchen *and* I also needed to eat, this seemed to be simpler." He placed two plates on the table—one in front of her and the other in front of the chair across from her—each one with a Western omelet that was big enough for three people to share. "What would you like to drink? I have orange juice, milk or coffee—it's decaffeinated."

She pushed her chair away from the table. "I can—"

"Stay seated. I'll get it."

"Thank you. Coffee, please."

"I'm sorry I don't have any of those fancy flavored creamers, but I have regular cream and sugar." He reached into the cabinet above the coffeemaker and removed two mugs.

"Just cream. Thank you."

He poured coffee into each mug and added a generous serving of cream to one of them. After setting the coffee with cream in front of her, he settled into his chair. "Do you mind if I say grace?"

"Kind and most holy Heavenly Father, we come to You this day to thank You for our many blessings. We especially thank You, Lord, for watching over Jenna and protecting her from the attacks on her life. I pray they capture her attacker, and if it's Your will, that she finally gets answers about her daughter's death. Please watch over us and keep all involved in this investigation safe from harm. Thank You for this food. I pray it's nourishing to our bodies. In Christ's name, amen."

Sean smiled at her, cut a generous piece of the omelet with the edge of his fork and took a bite. "Mmm. Go ahead. Try it." He pointed with the handle of the fork.

She poked at the omelet. Chunks of ham, bell pepper, onion and tomatoes spilled onto the plate.

"Is everything okay?"

Biting her lip, she lifted her eyes to meet his. "Why did you say 'if it's Your will' in the prayer? Why wouldn't God want me to have answers concerning Becca's death?"

Sean put his fork down, placing it on his plate, and wiped his mouth with a napkin. "I want to tell you that, yes, God wants everything about Becca's death to be revealed to you, but no one can know that for sure. I believe, one thousand percent, that He wants murderers to be captured and punished. However, even if you never find out who was behind Becca's death, God knows. And one day that person will face the ultimate judgment."

Jenna chewed on her bottom lip as tears stung the backs of her eyes. Why had she questioned his prayer?

For the same reason she'd been questioning God since her daughter died. Because without knowing who killed her beautiful Becca, she needed someone to blame. She looked down at her plate and forked a bite into her mouth. The eggs were pillowy—soft but tasteless. The food went down the wrong way, throwing her into a coughing fit. She reached for her cup and drank a large gulp, the hot liquid burning her already-dry throat.

Sean jumped to his feet and filled a glass with cool water from the dispenser on the refrigerator door. "Here." He placed the drink in her hand.

Jenna guzzled it like a person rescued after a week stranded in the desert.

"Slow down," Sean urged as he patted her upper back. "Are you okay?"

Placing the glass on the table, she felt heat creep up her neck. "I'm fine… Thank you," she said, her voice raspy. "I just took too big of a bite."

He didn't question her logic but raised an eyebrow.

"Really, I'm fine."

"Would you like me to fix you something else to eat?"

"No!" She puffed out a breath and picked up her fork. "No. Thank you. This is good."

He settled back into his seat, eyeing her. She took a few small bites. With each one, the omelet tasted better and better. Before she knew it, she'd eaten the entire thing.

Looking up, she noted that Sean had also cleaned his plate. She offered him a wobbly smile. "Thank you for the meal. It was delicious."

"You're welcome." The washing machine emitted three short beeps. "Sounds like the clothes are ready to go into the dryer."

Jenna scooted her chair back and crossed into the small laundry alcove, thankful for the distraction. Jenna transferred the clothing to the dryer, closed the door and pressed the start button. Turning back to the kitchen, she saw Sean had already cleared the table and was in the process of loading the dishwasher.

"Here, let me do that. You cooked. I should at least do the cleanup."

"That's not necessary. Besides, I'm almost finished." He placed the last few dishes onto the rack, dropped a detergent pod into the dispenser, clicked the door closed and started up the machine. Then he grabbed a sponge off the sink and began wiping everything down. "I left our mugs on the table. Why don't you pour us both another cup of coffee?"

As much as she'd love to go hang out in the guest room until he went to the camper for the evening, she didn't think it would be polite to argue. She snagged the coffeepot off the warming plate and began refilling the cups at the table.

"Done," Sean declared. "I'll be right back. I want to grab a notebook and pen from my office. Then we can sit at the table and you can tell me everything you know about Becca's murder."

Startled, Jenna glanced up and sloshed coffee onto the wooden tabletop. "Oh, no." She returned the coffeepot and reached for the roll of paper towels she'd seen on the counter, but Sean had already grabbed them and wiped up her mess.

He turned to her with concern in his eyes. "You didn't get burned, did you?"

"No, I'm fine. Just embarrassed." She struggled not to squirm under his gaze.

"There's nothing to be embarrassed about. Accidents happen." Leaning against the counter, he folded his arms across his chest. "If you're not up to discussing your daughter's case at the moment, we can wait and talk about it in the morning."

"Why do you want to go over the details? Do you think you can solve a case that the local authorities haven't?"

"I'm not sure. One thing I know is that I'm a very good detective. I also know the only way we can figure out who is trying to kill you is to solve your daughter's case."

Unable to form words around the lump in her throat, she nodded and settled into the chair she had sat in earlier, wrapped her hands around the warm coffee mug and tried to ward off the chill that engulfed her. Feeling judged and being the brunt of other people's jokes were two things that had always bothered her. While she didn't suspect Sean would make jokes at her expense, she had felt judged by him many times over the last six months when he'd driven past with a frown and a shake of his head as she cleaned up whatever mess vandals and anti-fans had made of her yard and the exterior of her home.

Jenna had longed for someone to discuss the case with, someone who would tell her if they thought she was on the right trail or not and would give her their take on the leads she'd uncovered. But she'd hoped that person would be a supportive friend. She met Sean's gaze and slowly released her breath. "I doubt I'll sleep much tonight anyway, so let's discuss it now."

"I'll be right back." He took off down the hall and ducked into a room at the back of the house.

Lord, please, let Sean figure out what we've all been missing. It's time for Becca's murderer to be put away so he can't hurt anyone else ever again.

Sean crossed to the walnut desk that sat in front of the built-in bookcases in the room that had been his grandfather's office but was now his. He moved behind the desk, rolled the chair aside, pulled open the middle drawer and rummaged around until he found an ink pen. Then he closed the drawer and snatched the spiral notebook off the corner of the desk, knocking over the small black picture frame that housed a photo of him and Felicia taken on their nineteenth anniversary.

He picked up the frame and examined the photo. It was his favorite picture of the two of them. While Felicia beamed at the photographer, Sean had turned away from the camera to smile at his beautiful wife. She had always been his favorite view, and he was thankful she had insisted on having professional photos taken to commemorate their anniversary that year.

He'd tried to persuade her to wait until their twentieth anniversary, since nineteen wasn't a milestone. She'd laughed and said, "Every year I get to spend with you is a blessing, and I intend to celebrate all our anniversaries as if they are the most important day of the year. Because to me, they are."

So he had agreed to an outdoor photo shoot in Piedmont Park. Three weeks later, the day after Felicia had been murdered, the photographer emailed the digital file of the photos to their joint home email account.

"Are you okay?"

He startled at the sound of Jenna's voice and looked up to see her in the doorway. "Yeah. I'm fine."

Jenna walked over to him and craned her neck to see the picture in his hands. "Your wife was beautiful. I don't know if I've ever told you, but I'm sorry for your loss."

"Thank you." He put the photo back on his desk where it belonged. "She passed a long time ago."

"Doesn't mean you don't still miss her," Jenna replied softly.

He didn't want to discuss his feelings over the loss of his wife with Jenna—or the frustration he'd felt over the dead-end leads they'd received on the tip hotline, mainly thanks to all the crime scene investigator wannabes on social media. Sean held up the notebook and pen. "I got what I was looking for. Why don't we go back to the kitchen table so we can be comfortable?"

Not waiting for her reply, he brushed past her and headed down the hall toward the kitchen. It was nearing eight o'clock. If he hoped to get all the facts straight and retire to the camper before midnight, he needed to keep them focused on the topic at hand. What had Jenna uncovered about her daughter's murder that had turned the killer's attention on her? And if the killer thought the information was enough to convict them, why hadn't the police discovered it already?

He selected the chair next to hers instead of the one on the other side of the table. One thing he'd learned as a detective was that sometimes you had to sit elbow to elbow to get to the nitty-gritty details. Building camaraderie couldn't be achieved if the parties involved in the investigation were standoffish to each other.

Jenna dropped an expandable file folder onto the table

with a thud. "These are all my notes. I have everything backed up on my computer, but I like to keep hard copies, too."

Sean picked up the folder. Instead of choosing one that was a generic brown color, she had chosen one with flowers and a hummingbird design imprinted on it. In all his years with the police force, he'd never seen clues stored in such a colorful vessel. He cleared his throat and unlatched the folder, which appeared to be stretched to its limit. "I'm glad you thought to pack this when we stopped by your house."

"There's no way I'd let this out of my sight. I kept it locked in a fire-resistant filing cabinet in my home office." She dropped into the seat beside him and settled her laptop onto the table in front of her. She flipped it open and pressed the power button. "I thought we might want to watch the video from my last podcast recording where I talked about Becca's case."

"What other cases do you discuss on your podcast? Do you stick to cold cases that the police have already given up on?"

"Sometimes I'll touch on a murder that has recently happened." Her fingers flew over the keyboard as she typed in her security code. "I started out just talking about Becca's case, trying to keep it in the news so the police wouldn't forget it—"

"Police don't forget cases, especially ones that involve young people. And I can promise you, murder cases they can't solve plague them." It had always bothered Sean when people thought that because a case wasn't solved, the police didn't care.

"I—" Jenna bit her lower lip. "Sorry. Poor choice of

words. I believe, in the beginning, Sheriff Rice wanted to solve this case. But after several months, he hit upon the idea that Becca had committed suicide and, after that, quit trying."

"Where is Sheriff Rice now?"

"He moved to the Gulf Coast after he retired." She sighed. "A high-profile serial killer case happened here the year before Becca… Sheriff Rice never explicitly stated it, but I think when they discovered Becca's body, he was afraid it was another serial killer. Thankfully, no other young women came up missing, so it quickly became obvious that wasn't the case."

As he took a sip of lukewarm coffee, flashes of days gone by flooded his mind—being buried in a case, sifting through clues, and surviving on cold coffee and junk food. It had gotten especially bad after he'd lost Felicia. Sean had hated going home to an empty house and had spent days on end at the station. He'd convinced himself he was the only one who could solve her case, so he couldn't go home to shower, sleep or eat.

Until the day—five months after Felicia's murder— Chief Monica Freeman had told him if he didn't leave the station for a minimum of eight consecutive hours each day, she'd have no choice but to suspend him. He'd said some not-so-nice words in reply and stormed out. Thankfully, she'd understood he was coming from a place of pain and wasn't intentionally lashing out at her. And she'd called her husband—Sean's former high school track coach— and sent him to Sean's house to check on him. When Coach Freeman had arrived, he took one look at Sean and told him to take a shower. Then he'd taken him out for a big steak and a long talk.

It hadn't gotten much easier to go into his home afterward. But that night, Sean had slept better than he had in months, and the next morning he'd packed his camping gear and taken off for a week of intense hiking in the North Georgia mountains, giving him much needed time for prayerful thoughts on moving forward without the love of his life by his side.

He looked from the bulging file folder in his hand to the beautiful woman peering at her computer screen. One didn't have to be a detective to deduce she'd had no one to talk sense into her like Coach Freeman had him—or if she had, she hadn't taken their advice.

Dear Lord, forgive me for not realizing what Jenna needed wasn't someone to tell her to stop her podcast, but rather someone who would help her realize racing through life, putting herself in danger, wouldn't bring Becca back. Someone who would encourage her to take time for self-reflection, so she could develop a plan to move forward and have a full life, even while missing the one she loves the most.

Could Sean be that person for Jenna? Or had he already botched any chance to be a friend she would take advice from? He puffed out a silent breath. Before he could ever hope to be the friend to her that his former track coach had been to him, he'd have to solve her daughter's four-year-old cold case murder.

FIVE

Unable to fully turn off his mind and rest, Sean had been up for hours, pacing and fighting the urge to go inside and look through Jenna's files in greater detail. He scrubbed a hand over his stubbled cheek. It was barely past 6:00 a.m., but he couldn't stand the thought of staying in the camper a minute longer. He needed coffee and Bible time, and Beau was probably eager to get outside to stretch his legs and take care of business.

If he tread lightly, Sean should be able to enter through the back door without waking his guest. He'd let Beau outside, put on a pot of coffee and settle into his favorite chair for his scripture reading and prayer time. After that, he'd feed Beau and dive back into the file Jenna had composed on her daughter's death.

He stepped out into the frosty morning, pulled the camper door closed and made his way to the back of his farmhouse, his breath sending small puffs of fog into the air. Playful barking reached his ears, and he looked up just as Beau leaped at him. "Whoa, boy, what are you doing outside?" He scratched behind the coonhound's ears and bent close for their usual sloppy morning kisses.

The smell of coffee and bacon greeted Sean as he pushed

open the back door. Jenna sat at the table, her brow furrowed as she wrote in a notebook.

"Good morning. The coffee is hot, and there's toast and bacon staying warm in the oven." Jenna pushed to her feet. "I'm happy to make you some eggs if you'll tell me how you like them cooked."

He waved her off. "No need. Continue with what you were doing. I can fix my breakfast after I feed Beau."

She settled back into her seat. "I hope it was okay that I let him outside. He was scratching at the back door."

"Yeah, it's fine. He's good to stay nearby, especially when it's feeding time." Sean reached into the dog-food storage container that sat just inside the pantry, scooped up a serving and carried it out to the sunroom with Beau on his heels.

After depositing the food into the metal dish next to the water bowl near Beau's bed, he returned to the kitchen, washed his hands and poured himself a cup of coffee. Then he took a seat beside Jenna and reached for the notepad he had used the night before. Jenna had sketched out a timeline of events of Becca's last day, using cell phone–location records and bank records that she had gathered over the years.

"Have you ever physically retraced Becca's steps from that day?" Before she could answer, he rushed on. "I'm not asking if you have been to the places she visited that last day. What I'm asking is, have you retraced her steps, going to each location in one day, following her timeline as closely as possible?"

"No. I *have* been to the locations, all of them. I questioned the people that worked with her at the library and the people at the café. But I've never retraced her steps the way you're talking about." Her brow furrowed, and she turned to him. "Do you think it would make a difference?"

"I'm not sure. It's just a thought that came to me." Sean took a sip of his coffee, checked the time on the stove's clock and glanced at the paper in his hand. "According to the timeline, Becca left home around seven thirty in the morning, headed to her part-time job at the library, where she worked from eight until two. It's a little after seven now. I don't think that we need to hang out at the library for six hours. So why don't we listen to your last two podcasts and leave here around eleven?"

"Okay. But if it's all the same to you, I'd prefer if we listen to the podcasts separately." She closed her laptop. "I'll go to the bedroom. That way, you can stay in the kitchen and eat while you listen to it on your phone."

"What if I have questions? Wouldn't it be better to listen to it together?" He watched as she continued to gather her things.

"No. The podcasts only last about forty-five minutes each. Since we're only listening to the last two, we'll have plenty of time for a question-and-answer session afterward." Jenna turned and hurried out of the room.

Shaking his head, he pushed away from the table, picked up his mug and went over to the coffeepot for a refill. Then he pulled up the podcast on his phone, hit play and placed the device on the counter beside his mug. The intro music to the podcast started playing as he took eggs, cheese and butter out of the fridge. He felt as if he was at a disadvantage. She could escape his presence, but with her voice filling the room, he couldn't escape hers.

Why hadn't she stayed in the kitchen with him? Was she afraid of what he would think of the episodes? Man, he'd really messed up with his criticism in the early days of their acquaintance. Felicia had warned him many times that his matter-of-fact personality could be off-putting. He should have listened to her and learned to be more tactful.

"Lord, we're commanded to love our neighbor. I never intended to put strife between us. My instinct has always been to protect, and I couldn't get past the thought that she was putting herself in harm's way. Or that she might be hindering the investigation, enabling a killer to remain free. But it was thoughtless of me to tell her she was wrong when we didn't know each other well enough for me to voice an opinion."

Sean cracked an egg into a small bowl and resolved to make amends with his neighbor. The fastest way to do that would be to solve her daughter's murder. Pulling his attention back to the podcast, he whisked the eggs and poured them into the hot frying pan.

Jenna powered off her computer and plodded to the door. Pulling it open an inch, she listened.

"I'm starting to wonder if the letter *T* Becca had written in her datebook wasn't referencing Thatcher Park, where they found her car, but it was the initial of the name of the person she was meeting," her voice echoed in the silence.

It sounded like Sean had approximately ten minutes remaining on the podcast. Good. This would give her a little more time before she had to face him. She silently closed the door, turned back to the room and hefted her suitcase onto the bed. If they were going to retrace Becca's steps, she'd need to change into a warmer sweater.

She chewed her lower lip. Would he, once again, try to convince her to give up the podcast? Did it really matter if he did? Her own mother and sister had told her to give up the podcast and go back to work, but she didn't want to be a high school guidance counselor anymore. The thought of being around all the students—who were the same age Becca had been when she died—preparing to go out into the world and live their dreams made her stomach twist into knots. She couldn't—no, she *wouldn't*—do it. Even after they had solved Becca's murder. There were too many grieving families that deserved closure. Jenna would continue to be their vocal advocate.

There was a light rap on the door.

"I made a fresh pot of coffee. Come on out whenever you're ready," Sean said from the other side.

She moistened her lips. "I'll be right there."

Jenna heard him turn and leave and listened until his footsteps faded. After pulling an emerald green cable-knit sweater out of her suitcase, she tugged it on over her head. Then she sat on the edge of the bed, pulled on a pair of thick wool socks and shoved her feet into her hiking boots. After tying the laces, she took a deep breath and stood. Time to see what clues Sean had picked up on that she may have missed.

"Lord, if You're listening, I'd appreciate it if Sean isn't critical in his assessment." *Ugh.* She shook her head. Why would she even pray for that? God gave everyone free will. He wasn't in heaven controlling people like puppets on a string. The way Sean portrayed his opinions would be his own choice. And the way she reacted would be Jenna's choice. "Lord, we both know I'm rusty at communicating with You. But if You wouldn't mind, please help me to hear Sean's thoughts without judgment and to temper my reaction. Thanks."

Jenna ambled down the hall and into the kitchen. "Sorry I kept you waiting."

"Not at all." He smiled at her. "You were smart to dress warmly for our day."

"Thanks."

"Would you like a travel mug for your coffee?"

She shook her head. "No. I'll just have half a cup before we go. Any more and I'll be wired all day."

He poured some of the hot black liquid into her cup, and she added a splash of creamer. "Thanks."

"You're welcome." Sean returned the coffeepot to the burner. "Thank you for cooking this morning. It was nice having bacon already prepared."

"It was nothing." Jenna fidgeted with her mug. The polite exchanges were wearing thin. "Can we discuss the podcast now? I'd like to know what you think triggered the recent attacks on me."

Sean sat in the chair across from her, took a sip of coffee and then placed his mug on the table. "First, I owe you an apology."

Of all the things he could have said, she hadn't been expecting that. "It's ok—"

"No," Sean cut her off. "It's not okay. I was rude. I judged you, and for that, I'm sorry."

"Thank you. I appreciate that."

He picked up the notepad. "I jotted a few thoughts down. It seemed like you only shared details the police had—I'm guessing—already shared with the public, but with your unique take on the details. Is that correct?"

"Yes." She clasped her hands in her lap. "I never want to do anything that would jeopardize any future court cases. So I shared all clues I discovered with the police before I shared them on my podcast."

"Including the idea that the letter *T* was a person's initial?" He pinned her with his gaze.

"Well, no. But that wasn't really a clue. It was me simply brainstorming ideas. If I had a specific name in mind, I would have taken it to the police before mentioning it on my show. I didn't." She gasped. "You think I'm on to something, don't you?"

He shrugged. "It seemed to be the only *new* piece of information concerning Becca's case in your last episode. It's logical to think it could be what prompted the attacks. Which would mean your idea that *T* references a person wasn't too far-fetched."

If *T* was a person, figuring out a name wouldn't be a simple task. Her heart thundered in her chest. Barton Creek was a small town. Making a list of *T* names would be time consuming but not difficult. However, since Becca had worked in Maryville, a college town, tracking down all the people she had come in contact with would be pretty much impossible.

"Don't feel defeated before we even get started. I know this is an enormous task," Sean said as if he'd read the doubt on her face. "But you're not working alone anymore. You have me to help. And I don't give up easily."

She raised an eyebrow. "After all these months of telling me I'm being reckless, why are you so willing to help all of a sudden?"

"Because your life is in danger."

"It's my own fault. You warned me that if I didn't stop digging and poking, it would be," Jenna whispered.

"Actually, it's partly my fault, too."

"What?"

"I could have been less blunt with my words. It's a trait I need to work on." He closed the notepad and clicked the pen closed.

"If I had voiced my concerns differently, you may have listened. But even if a different approach hadn't deterred you from the course you chose, I could have been a better neighbor by offering to help you solve the case sooner. I can't go back in time and change my bluntness or my un-neighborly actions." Sean locked eyes with her and held out his hand. "If you're willing to start over, I promise to be a good friend and a better neighbor. And I will not turn my back on you in a time of need again."

Tears stung the backs of Jenna's eyes, and she fought to hold them at bay. She had tried to convince herself not to take her neighbor's comments seriously in the early days of their acquaintance, but if she were truly honest with herself, she had taken every word to heart. And they had cut deep. Which made no sense, given that Sean was one in a long line of people who'd dismissed her through the years. Patrick turning his back on her, and her mom and sister doubting her ability to earn a degree while raising a child alone, had been just the beginning. Along the way, people had tried to introduce her to potential husbands because being a single mom would be too hard, and even Sheriff Rice hadn't taken her daughter's death seriously. Jenna should be used to doubters by now.

She swallowed past the lump in her throat, nodded and accepted his handshake. It would be nice to have someone working with her to decipher the clues. Who better than one of Atlanta's finest detectives? And maybe once this was all over, they could be real neighbors, who waved in passing and greeted each other in public. But even if this was simply a temporary truce, it would be worth it if he helped her capture Becca's killer.

SIX

Sean unlocked his SUV and opened the door for Jenna to slide into the passenger seat. They had spent the past hour at the library questioning the employees and volunteers but had learned nothing new.

"Thank you," she mumbled, a frown marring her face.

"Hey, now, don't become discouraged yet. This was our first stop. And you knew it was a long shot that anyone would have new information." He closed the door and jogged around the front of the vehicle.

After he settled into his seat and fastened his seat belt, he turned to face her. "Where to next?"

"Reba's Roadside Grill on Highway 33." Jenna flipped open the notebook and consulted the timetable. "But we're a little ahead of schedule. Becca phoned in the to-go order and arrived at two fifteen to pick it up. It's only one thirty now."

He shrugged, turned the key in the ignition and started the engine. "It's about a twenty-minute drive. We'll drive there now, then place our to-go order. By the time it's ready, our timeline should be in sync."

"Okay." She turned and stared out the window, effectively cutting off further discussion.

Sean drove in silence. He couldn't imagine how difficult this task was for Jenna. He'd never had to retrace Felicia's steps the last day of her life. The person who gunned down Felicia had done so in their driveway, in what he had thought was a safe suburb outside of Atlanta, where his enemies wouldn't find him. What he'd failed to factor in was that with today's technology, no one's address was safe from exposure. People with a grudge could always find their target. And the quickest way to exact revenge on Sean and bring him to his knees had been to kill Felicia. Right in front of him.

"Are you okay?" Jenna asked softly, pulling him from his thoughts.

"Yeah. Why do you ask?"

"You just sighed. And it was one of the saddest sounds I've ever heard."

"Oh." He wasn't purposefully trying to be evasive, but how did one respond to something like that?

They continued in silence for several more miles. The passenger seat squeaked as Jenna shifted to turn sideways and look at him. Refusing to squirm under her assessment, he bit the inside of his left cheek and focused on the road ahead.

"I know our truce—or friendship, or whatever you want to call the stage we're in right now—is still new, so I apologize if I'm being pushy or forward…"

"But?"

"Jim and Lois never said what happened to your wife. Just that she died suddenly."

Sean's breath caught, and he waited for her to continue.

"I was wondering…would you share the details of her murder with me?"

It was a fair question. After all, he knew as much about

her daughter's death as she did. Except he hadn't spoken about Felicia's murder with anyone other than his superiors and the officers who'd worked on her case. His in-laws, parents and grandparents had only known that she had been killed in a drive-by shooting—not the details. At least, not until the case went to court, at which time his grandparents had already died in a car crash. Sean silently released the breath he'd been holding.

"It was a Saturday afternoon. The day of the SEC Championship football game. The University of Georgia versus Alabama. We had lost to Bama during the regular season, and I was looking forward to the rematch. Felicia wanted to run some errands that morning. She'd asked me to accompany her. But despite her promise that we would be home in plenty of time for the big game, I refused to go."

His throat tightened as he recalled the annoyance in Felicia's voice when she'd accused him of always being too busy to spend time with her. He'd huffed and informed her that no husband would choose to go shopping with their wife that day instead of staying home to watch the pregame show.

If only he could go back in time and redo that one day, he would choose to spend it doing whatever she wanted without complaint.

"I would hazard a guess that ninety percent of the football-watching population would've done the same."

"I know." He clenched his teeth, and his jaw muscle twitched.

"Sorry. I wasn't trying to be flippant. There's nothing anyone can say that will ever take away your pain."

"I imagine you understand the pain better than most. And for the record, I did not take your comment as *flip-*

pant." He wanted to tell her that he knew what had happened to Felicia wasn't his fault, but he couldn't. Because it was. "You're right—most football fans would have probably done the same that day. My mistake was forgetting my choice of career would make both myself and my wife a target."

Jenna touched his arm. "You don't have to tell me more. I shouldn't have asked. It's none of my business."

"You're wrong. You have every right to ask." He spared a quick glance in her direction. "I have asked you to relive every detail of your daughter's death, and I'm even taking you on a road trip to revisit her last day."

"There is a notable difference, though. The details that I've shared are public knowledge. Shared by the police. And myself, on my podcast. I bared my grief to the world. You didn't. It was wrong to ask you to share it with me." She pulled back and clasped her hands in her lap.

Sean realized he wanted to tell her about the darkest day in his life—no, he *needed* to tell her—though he wasn't sure why.

"After she completed her shopping, Felicia picked up snacks for us to enjoy while we watched the big game. She called me when she turned on our street and asked if I'd come outside to help carry in the grocery bags. The game was starting in ten minutes, and she didn't want to miss the kickoff." He stopped at a four-way stop, then turned left.

"I didn't want to go outside in my house shoes, so I changed into a pair of sneakers. By the time I got outside, Felicia was standing behind the vehicle with the trunk open. She pulled out a pizza box from my favorite restaurant, lifted the lid and turned to me with a smile… She'd had the restaurant spell out *I Love You* with black olives. My anger evaporated, and the kickoff no longer mattered. The outcome of a game is a temporary feeling of elation or sadness, and wasn't nearly as important as our marriage. And I was about to tell her so when a car stopped at the curb. I turned to see who it could be. The guy in the passenger seat was a gang member whose wife I'd helped put away for peddling drugs at an elementary school. The instant I saw the glint of the gun barrel, I yelled for Felicia to get down and raced toward her. But before I could reach her, three shots rang out, and she crumpled to the ground in a pool of blood."

Jenna gasped.

"Sorry. I shouldn't have been so graphic."

"No. It's fine," she said, her voice cracking. "I just... I didn't know she had been killed in front of you. I'm sorry."

Sean pressed his lips together. Her words were meant to convey sympathy, but it felt more like pity. Sean *had* witnessed Felicia getting shot in front of him, and he hadn't done anything to prevent it. When she'd needed him most, he failed her.

Reba's Roadside Grill came into view, and he slowed the vehicle. "We have arrived." And none too soon. Sean needed to refocus Jenna's attention to the task at hand— solving Becca's murder and figuring out who was trying to kill Jenna—and off his biggest failure as a husband *and* a police officer.

Jenna took a bite of her cheeseburger, and a combination of grease and condiments slid down her chin. She quickly pulled a napkin out of the white paper sack and wiped the mess away before it could drip onto her sweater. "I don't think there's a graceful way to eat this burger."

"No." Sean swallowed and smiled. "But that's what makes it so good. This is the best burger I've had in a long time. Why hasn't anyone told me about Reba's before?" He took another bite. "Yum."

He was right. It was the best burger for miles around. She'd always thought so. Only today, it tasted like soggy cardboard. She eyed her partially eaten meal, wrapped it back up and placed it in the bag. Then she took a big sip of her sweet tea and scanned their surroundings. Sean had parked exactly where she'd told him they'd found Becca's car. They were in a remote area of the park, near a meditation garden a local doctor had built in memory of his late wife. Most people parked closer to the playground and the walking trail.

"Who could Becca have met here?" she mused aloud. "My gut is telling me it had to be someone important. But why meet here?"

Sean reached for his cola and took a big gulp; then he put it back in the cup holder. "How old was Becca at the time of her death? Eighteen?"

"Seventeen."

"If it was a guy she met that day, I'd imagine she met him here for the same reason any teenage girl would meet up with a guy for an afternoon picnic in a remote area. She liked him."

Jenna gasped. "No." She furrowed her brown. "I'm sure you're wrong. Becca wasn't like most girls. She had a good head on her shoulders when it came to boys and relationships, choosing to go out just in groups. And as friends only."

Sean tilted his head and pinned her with his gaze. "I've never known a teenager who wasn't interested in dating. Not saying they don't exist, but I'd say they're a rare group."

"Becca had a long-term plan to earn her college degree and get firm footing in her career before she married." Clasping her hands in her lap, Jenna found herself once again fighting the urge to squirm under his gaze. Becca was unique, and Jenna would not apologize for discouraging her daughter from following in her footsteps and marrying young. She'd wanted more for her child than to be a single parent in her early twenties. Her wish had been for her to live her dreams without regrets. Jenna had wanted Becca to…live life to the fullest. But now she was dead.

Had Jenna's desperate desire for her daughter to have the *perfect* life pushed Becca into secretly meeting a boy who then killed her? The backs of Jenna's eyes stung. She bit her cheek, but there was no stopping the flow of tears. Turning her head so her long brown hair hid her face, she feverishly scrubbed the tears away with one hand.

Sean pressed a napkin into her free hand. "I'm sorry. I didn't mean to upset you," he said, his voice remorseful.

Heat crept up her neck. "It's not your fault." She wiped her face with the napkin, then quietly blew her nose. Turning toward him, she frowned. "It just hit me that I forced my desires onto Becca. If she secretly met a boy, it was because she didn't think she could be open with me about liking him. It's my fault she's…dead." The dam broke, and tears poured down her face.

"It is not your fault. You can't blame yourself for someone else's actions." Sean twisted sideways and pulled her into a hug. "Ouch," he mumbled and shifted a little closer.

She pulled back and looked at his face, which was contorted in pain. "Steering wheel?"

"Yeah. Sorry."

"Why? For trying to offer comfort to a crying mother and injuring yourself in the process?" Settling into her seat, she dried the remaining tears and released a shuddered breath.

"I didn't expect to have this kind of reaction coming here today. I don't know what has come over me. Actually, that isn't true." Jenna pulled her left leg underneath her and turned to face Sean. "What you said about Becca meeting a guy... I had convinced myself her decisions about dating and earning a degree first had been her choice, but now I'm not so sure. If I'm the reason for those choices...and she met a guy she liked in secret to keep it from me...then it *is* my fault she's dead."

"Young people sometimes make bad choices. It doesn't mean their parents are bad people. Or that it's the parents' fault. It simply means the person who made the choice wasn't old enough or wise enough to think through the consequences. Sometimes even fully grown and extremely cautious people still get caught up in situations they never planned for." He picked up the take-out bag and dropped the remains of his meal into it before depositing it onto the passenger side floorboard at her feet. Then he pulled his seat belt around him, clicked it into place and met her gaze. "Ready to go to the next stop?"

A lump formed in her throat. The next stop was the hiking trail where Becca's body had been discovered. Jenna swallowed and reached for her own seat belt.

"If you don't think you can face any more today, we can go back to my house."

"And what? Continue to go over the notes in my files like we did last night? That's not getting us anywhere."

Sean dipped his head, turned the key in the ignition and backed out of the parking space. "While I drive, do you want to go over the list of classmates and friends that the police spoke to four years ago? Maybe you'll think of someone they missed."

She puffed out a breath and reached for the notepad, though she'd practically memorized all her notes. "They interviewed every member of Becca's graduating class. All seventy-three students. As well as any students in the other grade levels who had a class with her or interacted with her. They *all* had alibis that checked out."

"Okay, what about the teachers and staff?"

"Do you really think that a teacher is responsible? What would be the motive?"

"That, I do not know. However, if we can find someone who doesn't have an alibi and who someone saw with Becca the day she died, we could uncover the motive."

Jenna pulled a pen out of her purse, clicked it open and started doodling on the notepad. A thought materialized. "What if I've been looking in the wrong place all these years?"

"What do you mean?"

"If your theory is correct, and Becca met a boy for a picnic that day, then we have to consider it might not have been a classmate. Working at the library in Maryville, she could've met anyone. From a high school student to a college student to a much older man. And whoever it was could have moved far away by now." Jenna drew a big question mark on the paper, clicked the pen closed and shoved it along with the notepad back into her bag. "We might never find him."

"You're wrong. We will find him and stop him before he hurts you, too."

The muscle in his jaw twitched, again, and she balled her hand into a fist to keep from reaching out and touching it. Anger radiated off him. Was he that worried about her? Or was he simply upset that she had created this situation, putting him in a position to protect her?

"I… I appreciate all that you're doing to protect me. I'm sorry that my carelessness has caused this situation. If you want to drop me off at a rental-car location, I can rent a car and then you wouldn't need to drive me around."

"That's not happening." He glanced in her direction. "Do you really think I would abandon you now?"

She shrugged.

A frown briefly marred his face before he turned back to the road in front of him. Silence blanketed the vehicle.

Jenna hadn't meant to insult him or his integrity. She'd simply wanted to give him an out. Sure, he had volunteered to be her protector, but it had only been because he'd known the police force was not large enough to offer twenty-four-hour surveillance. And while he'd been great the night before, listening to her retelling of the facts pertaining to Becca's last day as she understood them, she knew he had to be annoyed that she hadn't listened to his advice to walk away from the podcast months ago. It had been her experience that when men found themselves in situations not of their choosing, they looked for a quick exit. Like Patrick had when they'd unexpectedly become young parents.

They arrived at the parking area for the hiking trail, and

Jenna reached into the back seat and grabbed her down jacket and quickly slid her arms into the sleeves. Then she grasped the small daypack, which held two bottles of water, protein bars and a first aid kit, climbed out of the SUV and turned toward Sean as he came around the back of the vehicle.

"Are you sure you want to do this?" he asked.

"What's my other choice? I doubt you'd let me stay in the vehicle alone. And by the time we could get Heath or another officer out here to babysit me, the sun will have dropped further in the sky, and it will be too dark for you to see anything." She headed toward the trailhead. "Come on. Like your grandma Lois would say, 'Daylight's burning.'"

Sean jogged to catch up to her, but she did not slow her pace. She might be several inches shorter than him, but she had mastered the skill of taking long, quick strides.

"How did you determine what time of day Becca arrived here?"

"Sheriff Rice actually came up with the timeline. He based it on the autopsy report. We knew what time Becca got off work and the approximate time she picked up the food from Reba's. Based on the digested state of the food in her stomach and how long it should have taken her to hike to Eagle Point, he estimated she arrived here between four thirty and five o'clock. Which would have given her an hour and a half to complete the two-mile loop."

"Was the sheriff able to locate any witnesses to corroborate his theory?"

She shook her head, and a strand of hair fell across her face. Tucking the hair behind her ear, she looked up at him. "It's not uncommon for this trail to miss a lot of the foot traffic from the Appalachian Trail. Even though they're connected, this trail is a little more off the beaten path. I will forever be thankful for the two hikers who actually hiked the trail that morning." She licked her lips. "Without them, there's no telling how long it would have been before her body was discovered."

Jenna faltered a step, and he grasped her elbow to steady her. Anger bubbled up inside, as it always did when she thought of someone pushing her daughter off a cliff and leaving her alone to die in the woods.

Jenna closed her eyes for the briefest of seconds and puffed out a breath, then looked back up at him. "Ready to follow in my daughter's last footsteps?"

"If you are."

She concentrated on walking along the narrow trail. When the curve in the trail came into view, she pointed. "Just beyond that point, we'll come to a Y. If we go left, the trail will take us up to the ridgeline to the outcropping of boulders known as Eagle Point, where Becca fell from. If we go right, the trail will lead us to the spot where they discovered her body."

"Let's go to the ridgeline first. Then we'll circle back around."

Jenna nodded and led the way. While she hadn't been able to make herself go to the top of the ridgeline before now, she'd been on the lower trail countless times in the past four years. Usually, she brought flowers to leave at the spot where her child had taken her last breath, but she hadn't wanted to seem silly or overly emotional to Sean, so she hadn't asked to stop to pick up a bouquet. She'd bring flowers next time. Today she was on a mission to gain closure on Becca's untimely death and to stop the killer before he killed her, too.

SEVEN

"What time of year was Becca mu—" Sean swallowed his words. He was a police veteran with thirty years of service. Why was he suddenly hesitant to call it what it was? A murder. Was it because Jenna had allowed herself to be vulnerable with him today? He'd seen a lot of women cry, but other than Felicia or his mom, none of their tears had tugged at his heartstrings the way Jenna's tears had earlier. He didn't know whether to be thankful or disappointed that the steering wheel had jabbed him and prevented him from embracing her.

Thankful. He *was* thankful. No need to blur the lines of neighborly friendship. While he didn't know if his beautiful, single neighbor was interested in finding a mate, or not, he knew without a doubt that he wasn't. Sean had already been married to his one and only love. She had rolled her eyes at his corny jokes and tolerated his constant stealing of the remote every Saturday. All while wearing a smile and making him feel like the most blessed man in the world.

"Spring."

He shook his head, pushing his thoughts aside. "What?"

Jenna stopped suddenly and spun around to face him,

a scowl on her face. "You wanted to know when Becca was murdered. Right? It was in the spring. April 17. Five weeks before her high school graduation." She jerked her head toward the trail on the left. "We're going this way."

"Would you rather lead or follow?"

"Lead." She pivoted and started up the slight incline.

Of course she wanted to lead. Sean didn't know if he had ever met a more independent woman. It was fine with him, though. He could take his time and take in the view of his surroundings without her questioning why he was snapping pictures of various things. He slipped his phone out of his back pocket and accessed the camera app. It wasn't like he expected to find earth-shattering clues four years after the fact, but one never knew where they might find a hint of something that another investigator had missed.

"You said the previous sheriff had unofficially classified Becca's death as a suicide. What were his reasonings?"

"Other than the fact that six months after Becca's death, he still didn't have any clues who the murderer was?"

"Come on, do you really think that's the only reason the idea of suicide came up?" He'd never met Sheriff Rice, since he had retired and moved to Florida before Sean moved to Barton Creek. But he'd heard stories about what a fair and dedicated lawman the sheriff had been.

She maneuvered around a tree branch that partially blocked the trail. "As far as I know, Matthew Rice was a good sheriff. But I don't think he wanted to leave office with an unsolved case. It was easier for him to believe it was suicide."

He understood Sheriff Rice not wanting to walk away

from his job with an unsolved murder. But twisting the narrative to fit what he wanted was unethical.

"Did he tell you why he suspected suicide?" Sean felt like a heel for pushing the issue, but he needed to understand every aspect of this case if he hoped to solve it.

"Becca and two of her closest friends had had a falling-out a couple of months earlier. When I tried to talk to Becca about it, she just said that their priorities had changed. When Sheriff Rice spoke to the girls, they told him that Becca had seemed depressed."

"Did you see any symptoms of depression in Becca?"

"No. I saw a child that was working hard to reach her goals. And while I never would've done such a thing while she was alive, after Becca passed away, I read her journal. The falling-out she'd had with her friends was because they were sneaking out of their homes at night and meeting boys they'd met online. They were partying and drinking. Becca told them what they were doing was wrong. That it wasn't right to worry their parents and that it was dangerous to meet strangers from the internet. They accused her of trying to be their conscience."

They reached the top of the ridge, and Jenna sat down on the bench at the overlook. "Was she sad and lonely without her friends? Yes. Was it enough to push her to kill herself? No. Her journal was full of her hopes and dreams and how much she was looking forward to college in the fall." A tear slid down her cheek, and she brushed it away. "Before she left for work the day she died, she made me promise that we'd go to the mall after church the next day and shop for her dorm room. That's not something someone contemplating suicide would be concerned with. Is it?"

The desperation in that simple two-word question almost brought him to his knees. He settled onto the bench beside her, his arm brushing against hers. "I wouldn't think so." Sean frowned. "And if it were suicide, why would someone be trying to kill you for poking around in the past?"

She gave a wry grin. "Who would have thought having someone trying to kill me would be a good thing? It proves Becca didn't commit suicide, and it means I'm getting close to the truth."

A bitter, icy wind blew through the trees, and Sean shuddered. The temperature had continued to drop steadily throughout the day. The weather forecast that morning had called for frost again overnight. He pushed to his feet and crossed to the wood-and-rock fence that stood about four feet high, separating the overlook from a rocky cliff that jutted out over the trail below. There were caution signs posted, warning hikers not to go beyond that point and to stay on the path. "Was the fence put up after Becca fell?"

"No. It's been here awhile. I think they built it when I was a freshman in high school. As I recall, there were some students who decided to have a late-night party out here to celebrate winning the state football championship. Two of the players fell off. One ended up with several cracked ribs, a broken arm and a broken ankle. It paralyzed the other guy from the waist down. The father of the paralyzed boy was the mayor, and three days later, there was a crew out here constructing the fence and posting warning signs." She came over to stand beside him and pointed at the sign. "That's another thing that has always puzzled me. The toxicology report didn't show any alcohol or sedatives in Becca's body. If her killer didn't drug her before tossing her off the cliff, how did he convince her to climb over the fence and hike out to the rocks? I can't imagine her willingly going along with that. She was a rule follower. And she was afraid of heights."

Sean didn't want to upset her more than he already had, but he could easily imagine someone holding a young girl at gunpoint—or knifepoint—and getting her to do his will.

Another thought struck. Had Becca's death really been murder? He furrowed his brow. Could it have been an accident? If it had been an accident, why hadn't the person with her come forward? Since Becca had left her car at the park to ride out here with the person she'd met, proving it was murder would have been harder than proving it wasn't. Unless... "I'm sorry to ask this, but were there any signs of forced trauma to Becca's body?"

"No. Thankfully, she wasn't...*violated*, if that's what you mean."

He pressed his lips together and nodded. "You sit here, but stay where I can see you. I'm going to climb those rocks and see if I can get any insight into what may have happened." He swung a leg over the fence.

She mimicked his move and pinned him with a glare. "I'm going with you."

"That's not a good idea." He searched her face. Her jaw tightened, and her eyes bore into his.

The sun dipped behind the trees, and it felt like the temperature had dropped ten degrees. If they wanted to get back to the car before the sun set completely, they had about an hour to look around and hike back to the lower trail to see where they had found Becca's body.

Lord, arguing with her will only cost me time, and I'm

sure it will be a losing battle. Please don't let her stubbornness cause her to be hurt.

"Okay. You can come, too, *but*…" He put a hand on her arm, ensuring he had her full attention. "You must follow my instructions every step of the way. I don't want you to get hurt."

A nervous laugh escaped her lips. "So, you *do* care what happens to me."

He scoffed. "Of course. I can't let anything happen to my grandparents' favorite neighbor. Besides, I can almost guarantee, if you die, the person after you will disappear, and we'll never find out who killed Becca."

"You have pinpointed exactly what has kept me alive and going all these years. I must find Becca's killer. And that is precisely why I'm going to be extremely careful out on the rocks." She climbed over the wood railing. "Are you coming?"

Dear Lord, my words didn't come out right. Of course Jenna's life is valuable. She's Your precious child. Please help her to see her worth so she won't give up on living once we finally solve this case.

A powerful gust of wind blew out of the southwest, and Jenna grasped a white oak tree. Her hair whipped across her face, but she refused to let go of the tree. A few more steps and she'd reach the tip of Eagle Point.

"Can you make it the rest of the way?" Sean placed a hand on her shoulder.

She puffed strands of hair out of her mouth. "The wind is stronger than I expected. I'll make it. I just need to get my balance first."

"Why don't you wait here? I'll go look around and be right back."

She shook her head. The rough bark scratched her cheek, and tears sprang to her eyes. She blinked them away. "No! I can do this."

For four years, this was the one place Jenna had avoided, too afraid to walk across the boulders to the spot where someone had tossed Becca's life away like yesterday's trash. Not today. Today, she would conquer her fears. After all, there was strength in numbers, and for the first time since that fateful April afternoon, Jenna had someone walking beside her. She was not alone.

An image of the cross-stitch tapestry her mother had given Jenna after her divorce came to mind: *Fear thou not; for I am with thee: be not dismayed; for I am thy God: I will strengthen thee; yea, I will help thee; yea, I will uphold thee with the right hand of my righteousness.* Isaiah 41:10.

Was it her own fault she'd walked alone all these years? How many people, including God, had she turned away, preferring to wallow in her grief? No, not preferring, but also not believing anyone could understand the depth of her pain. Every time her sister or mother had tried to tell her she needed to get out of her house and be around people—that she had to have a *life* to truly be alive—she had burrowed deeper into her shell. Then she'd recorded her first podcast and realized she could make a difference not just in her daughter's cold case but others too. Unfortunately, the decision had only pushed her further into her life as a loner. Not today. Today she was part of a team.

"You lead the way. I'll stay close behind." She released her hold on the tree.

Sean looked like he might argue, but then he pressed his lips together and moved ahead of her. "Okay. Hold on to the back of my jacket."

"No. Not that I plan to, but if I'm holding on to you and I slip, then we will both fall off the cliff."

He grasped her hand, his warm, callused fingers wrapped around hers. "I will not let that happen. Now, please, hold on to me."

Grabbing the back of his dark green Carhartt jacket with her left hand, she met his gaze. "Okay?"

"Thank you. Now, follow my steps."

Fighting to stay upright as they inched their way along the uneven surface, Jenna leaned into the wind. Six feet from the edge, she stepped on loose gravel, and one foot went out from under her. She landed on her backside with a thud. "Ouch!"

Almost at the same instant, a gunshot shattered the quiet afternoon, and a bullet hit the tree beside her, bark blasting through the air.

Sean crouched and crawled toward her. "Are you okay?"

"Yes." She shielded her eyes as she looked at where the bullet was embedded in the trunk, about level with where her head had been moments before.

Another explosion of gunfire sounded, this one hitting the boulder they were crouched on. Small bits of rock sprayed toward them. "What are we going to do? There aren't many places to hide out here."

"Follow me."

She followed closely behind him as they made their way to a nearby pine tree. The tree wasn't large enough for both of them to hide behind easily. Sean rolled onto his side, wrapped his muscular arms around her and dragged Jenna against him, her face buried in his chest.

Two more gunshots rang out, one hitting the tree in front of them and the other hitting the ground behind Jenna. She pulled back, and Sean pulled her close once more.

"I...can't...breathe," she said, her voice muffled by his winter jacket.

"What?" He shifted a few inches and looked down at her.

"I couldn't breathe." She puffed out a breath of air. "What are we going to do?"

Unzipping his coat, he reached inside and pulled out a handgun. "You're going to stay here while I try to get a clear shot and stop this guy."

He shifted his body, and she put a hand on his arm. "Be careful."

"Of course. Now, stay here." He pushed to his feet and ran to a boulder a few yards away. Another round of gunshots volleyed in their direction, a bullet hitting the large rock seconds after Sean had scooted behind it.

Jenna flipped onto her stomach and centered her body behind the tree, her eyes glued to Sean. He raised his gun and braced his arm on the boulder, pulling the trigger in rapid succession. And then silence. Several long minutes passed.

"Do—" Jenna swallowed the rest of her words when Sean shook his head, a finger pressed to his lips.

He crouched low and darted back to the tree where she waited. "I could see movement from a little higher on the ridge, but the person shooting was too far away for me to identify. I don't think he was expecting me to return fire."

"Where is he now?" She hoped she didn't sound as frightened as she felt.

"He disappeared in the trees. I think he's trying to get to a higher point so he'll have a better view. We have to get off this mountain."

"How do we do that? You don't know where the shooter is. He can pick us off like flies if we move out into the open. And if we make it to the trail, how can we be sure he isn't waiting for us there?"

Sean put his weapon into his shoulder holster. "Stay here. I'm going to look for another way down."

Jenna watched as he left the protection of the tree once again. She didn't know of any other trails or anything that would get them off the mountain more quickly than the one they had traveled to reach this point. Her heart raced. There was only one way off this rock. Over the edge. Straight down. The same way Becca had left Eagle Point.

They were trapped. All they could hope for was that the sun would set quickly and darkness would conceal their movements enough so they could escape. She didn't even want to think about how dangerous it would be to navigate the uneven ground they had covered to reach the pinnacle of the boulder that jutted out and over the path below in total darkness.

"Okay." Sean rushed back over to her, breathless. "On the other side of the boulder where I took cover, I found a small ledge about ten feet below us. And it looks like there's a narrow trail that winds its way from the ledge to the bigger trail below."

"A ten-foot drop?" she asked, aghast. "How do you expect us to drop ten feet without breaking a few bones?"

"I'm five-eleven."

"So?"

"I'll go first. If I maneuver correctly, the drop will be roughly four feet for me. Once I'm on solid ground, you mimic my steps, and I'll be there to catch you." He grasped her elbow and helped her to her feet. "Come on. Let's hurry."

His confidence did little to soothe her nerves. And she couldn't help but wonder if someone would find them and report their bodies or if they would be left for the wild animals to devour.

EIGHT

Sean spied a broken limb on the ground near the pine tree. It was about nine inches in diameter and six feet long. Would it be possible for Jenna to hold the limb over the edge of the cliff while he shimmied to the end of it and dropped to the ledge below? No. His weight would be too much, and the limb could break free of her grasp and swing up and smash her in the face. Maybe he could hang on to the root at the base of the tree and walk himself backward off the edge so he could control his drop. *Lord, please don't let me get injured. I can't leave Jenna in a position where she's not protected.*

"Pay careful attention, and watch my every move so you can mimic it once it's your turn." The fear that clouded her eyes was almost enough to make him tell her to forget it, they'd make a run for it. But he couldn't. If they stepped onto the open trail, they would be easy prey for the shooter. Their only hope was to get to the lower trail and make it harder for the shooter to see their movements. "I know you're afraid, but I wouldn't ask you to do this if I thought we had another option."

She bit her bottom lip. He leaned in. Catching himself, he stopped, his lips inches from hers. *What are you think-*

ing? You almost kissed her. Don't let the thought of not making it out of here alive make you do something you'll regret if—when—you survive. Get a grip.

"We *will* get out of here. Alive." he insisted, more confidently than he felt.

Jenna nodded. "Go. I'll be right behind you."

He rubbed his palms on his jeans, squatted and wrapped his hands around one of the larger roots that extended over the ledge below. "I'm going to use these roots to walk myself down the side of the mountain as far as I can. When it's your turn, do the same. I'll be there to catch you."

Jenna knelt beside him and covered his hands with hers. "I'm sorry I've put you in this situation."

"You didn't. The shooter did." He wanted to tell her much more. How he'd been wrong to judge her podcast. And that he regretted not being there for her as a neighbor. But this wasn't the time. "I'll see you at the bottom."

The root extended only about a foot down the side of the mountain, but every inch helped. When he reached the bottom of the root, he swung his legs out and dropped to the ground with a thud.

"Are you okay?" Jenna had lain on her stomach and was looking down at him.

"Yes. It wasn't that difficult." He held out his hands. "Your turn."

Sean watched as she grasped the root and copied his movements. She took two steps backward, lost her grip and plunged toward him. He braced for impact but had barely gotten his arms wrapped around her when they both fell back with a clunk.

Jenna rolled off him and helped him to sit up. "Did I hurt you?"

"No. I just need a...moment... To catch my...breath." He put a hand on his chest and took several slow, deep breaths. "Are you okay?"

She smiled. "Of course. I had a cushy landing."

"Are you calling me soft? I'll have you know, I'm solid mus—" The twinkle in her eye caught his attention. "You're laughing at me."

"No. Not at..." She sighed. "The counselor I saw after my divorce said making jokes when I'm anxious is one of my coping mechanisms. Sorry."

"Don't be. I cope with stress by whistling." He rubbed his jaw. "I've been biting the inside of my cheek to keep from whistling a tune."

A smile lit up her face, but she immediately replaced it with a somber expression. "So, what do we do now?"

"Now we follow that trail—" he pointed to the trail that hugged the side of the mountain where they stood "—and hope it leads us to the trail at the bottom of this mountain."

"I'll follow you."

A shiver raced up his spine. Her words reminded him of his conversation with Felicia when he'd told her he wanted them to move to a small town when he retired. She had insisted she could be happy anywhere as long as she was with him and that she would follow him "to the ends of the earth." Sean shook his head to clear his thoughts. They didn't have time to stand around.

"We need to move. Now." He grasped her hand, and an electric shock shot up his arm. When she tried to tug free, he wove his fingers through hers and held their clasped hands up. "I don't want us to get separated or for you to stumble and fall off the side of the trail." The explanation sounded flimsy even to his own ears, but he couldn't very well say that he was afraid of the shooter catching up with them and that he really needed the comfort of knowing she was safe.

She opened her mouth, then closed it and nodded.

Ducking under a dead vine, he started the slow descent with her at his heels. Fifteen minutes later, they reached the bottom trail. They hiked toward the parking area, and as they neared a curve in the path, a rustling noise to his right drew his attention. He dropped Jenna's hand and reached for his gun.

As they drew closer, they saw two helium balloons rubbing against each other in the wind. And on the ground, propped against a rock, was a bouquet of yellow roses.

"This is where Becca died. Who would leave flowers and balloons here?" Jenna caught the ribbon attached to one of the Mylar balloons. There was a floral image on the balloon, along with the words *I'm Sorry*. On the other balloon, one side read *You Are Loved, You Are Missed, You Are Remembered*; the other side read *Forever and Always*. She gasped. "Who? The murderer? What kind of game is he playing?"

Tears flowed down her face, and he pulled her into an embrace. "I don't know," he whispered against her ear. "I need to get pictures for the sheriff. Then we'll take everything with us and see if they can lift prints from any of it. Okay?"

She nodded. He pulled away from her and quickly snapped several photos. Then he pulled a small pocketknife out of his jacket pocket and punctured both balloons near the base. Once the helium had escaped, he quickly folded them—careful to only touch the edges—

and tucked them into his pocket. Then he knelt to get a closer look at the roses.

Seventeen long-stem yellow roses. One for each year of Becca's life. Wrapped in brown parchment paper and tied with a white bow. No card.

"What are you doing?" Jenna asked.

"Trying to figure out how to get these to the sheriff's office without getting my own prints all over the wrapper." He peered up at her. "Empty your backpack and give it to me."

She removed a couple of protein bars, sticking them in her back pants pockets, and then pulled two water bottles from the small daypack. He'd teased her earlier that they were only going on a short hike and wouldn't need the water and snack, but she'd just smiled. Now he was thankful for her foresight.

Jenna handed him the pack, and he slid the flowers into it, careful to touch only the rose stems and not the paper. Unable to zip up the bag with the long-stemmed flowers inside, he grasped the straps close to the top and stood.

"Do you want me to wear that?" Jenna nodded at the pack, a water bottle in each hand.

"No. I can carry it like this." He reached for a water bottle. "Thanks."

Sean flipped open the top and took a big gulp, then put it into the side pocket on the pack. "Ready to go?"

She glared at the roses peeking out of the backpack. "Yellow was her favorite color. Today was the first time I didn't bring flowers with me to leave at this spot… Why did he… How did he…" Her voice broke, and she pressed her lips together.

"I wish I had the answers. I don't. But we need to get a

move on before the shooter circles around and finds us." Tightening his hold on the daypack, he put a hand on the small of her back and urged her along. "What's the fastest time you've ever made it to your vehicle from this spot?"

"I don't know. Maybe twenty minutes."

"Can you shave five minutes off that time?"

"Do you think he's still out there?"

"I'm not sure, but I don't want to stick around and find out." He looked around at the dark shadows that surrounded them. "We're running out of daylight. We need to get to my vehicle."

"Follow me." She took off toward the trailhead, and he fell in step beside her.

They'd only gone a few feet when a gunshot rang out and a bullet hit the ground to their right.

"Run!" He grasped her hand and ran as fast as he dared on the rugged trail.

More gunfire sounded behind them.

"Here!" Jenna yelled, and pulled him off the trail and into the trees. "He won't be able to see us in here."

"True, but do you have any idea where you're going?" Sean inquired.

"Yes." Jenna darted behind a large tree and pressed against it, panting.

"That was smart thinking, running into the trees, but I'm glad we didn't break our necks."

"I know these woods. I've been out here so many times since Becca died. I believe I could navigate this section to the trailhead blindfolded if I had to."

"Thankfully, there's still a little daylight left. But only if we move fast."

He peered around the tree, searching for the shooter.

Jenna pointed. "There."

A shadow figure stood atop the rock overhang close to where they'd climbed down earlier. Sean watched as the figure turned and made his way back to the overlook at the ridge of the mountain. "Looks like he's headed back to the trail. Either he didn't see how we came off the mountain or he decided it was too risky to attempt in the waning sunlight."

"Let's go." Jenna took off at a brisk pace, and he had to jog a few steps to catch up to her.

They made it to his SUV in under fifteen minutes. There were no other vehicles in the area. The shooter must have parked at another location and hiked. Sean puffed out a breath. *Lord, I guess it was too much to hope the guy after Jenna was reckless enough to leave his vehicle in plain sight, but I need a break here. Something that will point me in the right direction. So I can solve this case before Jenna becomes a casualty.*

A sharp pain radiated behind Jenna's right eye and extended all the way to her temple. A migraine. She leaned her head against the passenger-side window, willing the cool glass to numb the pain. They had spent a couple of hours at the sheriff's office, giving their statements and answering questions. She was exhausted. Jenna planned to take pain pills and go straight to bed, when they arrived home. No, not home—Sean's house. She sighed. Would her life ever be normal again?

"That was a heavy sigh," Sean commented.

"I'm just tired. And I—" The words lodged in her throat. How could she complain about a headache and sore muscles? She was sure he was just as exhausted as she was.

And she had brought this attack on herself by sticking her nose in police business. Sean hadn't asked for it. He'd simply gotten caught in the middle of it by being in the wrong place at the wrong time.

"That's understandable. You've had a long day." He sped up. "I'll have us home soon. You can relax while I pop a pizza in the oven."

She didn't want pizza. The thought of food made her nauseated but more than that, she was desperate for space and time alone to process the events of the day. Only, how did one tell their host they didn't want to be in their company? Puffing out a silent breath, she rotated so more of her forehead touched the cool glass. Jenna looked out over Douglas Anthony's farm, which was lit only by the full moon above.

They were nearing her house. Oh, how she missed her bed, her recording studio, her comfortable sofa and fuzzy throw blanket she kept nearby. Maybe she could get Sean to stop by her house so she could pick up a few items she found comforting. No. She couldn't ask him to do that. Not tonight. But maybe she could go tomorrow and pick up a few things. She also needed to talk to Heath about finding alternate living arrangements.

Jenna was thankful for Sean and his hospitality, but finding the person who was after her could take weeks, months or even years. She couldn't continue to stay in his house, making him sleep outside in a cold camper. While they were at the sheriff's office, Heath had told her not to get her hopes too high that the fingerprints would come back with a match. Unless the person who'd killed Becca had a record, the likelihood of prints on file would be slim. And if the person was a serial killer, like the one who had shown up in Barton Creek the year before Becca's death, there would have been other murders after Becca's. While the constant dead ends were disheartening, Jenna was thankful no other mother in Barton Creek had lost a daughter the way she had.

Shifting in her seat, she caught sight of her house. Sitting back off the road, with the front window boarded up and no lights, the cozy home she'd tried to build for herself seemed depressing. Maybe it was time for her to consider moving to Nashville and getting a condo in the same complex as her sister, Amber. In a large city, she might remain in the shadows and avoid the person who was after her.

Was that a light inside her house? She forced her eyes to focus on the yellow glow in the guest room window. It was moving. "Stop the truck!"

Jenna turned and grabbed Sean's arm. "I saw a light. There's someone in my house!"

"What? Are you sure?" He slowed. "It could be the moon glinting off a window or something."

"No. Someone is inside my house with a flashlight. I saw it moving." She watched as they passed her home. Why hadn't he stopped the vehicle yet? "We need to catch him."

"If there's an intruder, I need to take you to my house. You can stay there with the doors locked and Beau to guard you. I'll come back alone." Sean sped up.

"But he'll get away. You know he had to have heard your vehicle and seen your headlights, too. Everyone in town knows there's only one house past mine on this road, so even if he can't see your SUV, he has to know we're the ones in this vehicle. He won't stick around and wait for you to come back and find him."

His brow furrowed. Good, he was thinking about her words.

"You have a weapon. And I'll stay behind you and follow your orders. Don't let him get away this time."

"Okay." He reduced his speed and pulled his SUV off the road, parking at the edge of her property where it joined his. Then he cut the lights, turned off the engine and shifted to face her. "Do you know how to drive a manual transmission?"

Why was he asking her about her driving ability? They were wasting time. She reached for the door handle, but he stopped her.

"You *will* stay inside this vehicle with the doors locked. Or we're both going to my house. Do you understand?"

Her irritation rose. She didn't need anyone giving her orders. She'd been taking care of herself for too many years. Only, he hadn't sounded demanding. Just concerned. Pressing her lips together, she nodded. "I understand."

He leaned close, his brow furrowed. "Can you drive my vehicle?"

"Yes."

"Okay, I'm leaving the keys. I want you in the driver's seat. Get out of here at the first sign of trouble. Got it?"

"Do you want me to call 911?"

"No." He reached up and turned off the dome light, then opened his door. "We don't know if the light you saw was a flashlight beam or not. There may be no one inside."

Jenna bit back the retort that itched to be released. She knew what she saw. But arguing about it would only prolong Sean's departure, giving the intruder a chance to escape. She crawled over the console and settled into the driver's seat he'd just vacated. "Be careful."

"Lock the doors." He dropped the keys into her outstretched hand, turned and jogged toward her house.

She pressed the door-lock button, her eyes trained on her yard. As Sean neared the front steps, a dark figure raced from the back of the house toward the tree line that hid the fence separating her property from Doug Anthony's farm.

Sean would be upset with her, but Jenna couldn't let the guy get away. He had to be stopped so she could move back into her home and live life again, and so she would finally have answers about Becca's death.

Throwing open the SUV door, she shoved the keys into her front pocket and charged into the night.

NINE

The hairs on the back of Sean's neck stood at attention at the sound of footsteps pounding across the front yard. He palmed his gun and spun around. And came face-to-face with Jenna. She gasped, her eyes wide with fear.

"I thought I told you to stay put," he whispered, slipping the gun back into its holster.

"The guy…" she panted, placing a hand on her chest as if to steady her heartbeat, "…ran out…the back door. Headed toward Doug's pasture."

"Get back to my vehicle and call Heath. I'll go after the intruder." Sean took off around the corner of the house, praying she'd follow his directions, though he suspected she wouldn't.

Lord, please protect her when I can't. The prayer he had prayed for Felicia every time he left for work slipped unbidden to his mind. "Lord, I failed Felicia. Please don't let me fail Jenna, too."

Felicia's smiling face flashed through his mind and was quickly replaced by an image of Jenna, sad and frightened out on the trail today. *Focus.* He pushed the thoughts away and pressed on toward the trees at the back of the property.

Pausing beside a beech tree, he listened. Silence. Where

had the intruder gone? A cloud drifted in front of the moon. He desperately wanted to use the flashlight function on his cell phone, but he couldn't risk giving away his location. A coyote yapped in the distance, and a dog barked in response. Had the intruder gone across Doug's pasture? Or was he hiding somewhere in the trees?

Frustration bubbled up. He had to have light if he hoped to capture the intruder. Palming his weapon in his right hand, he activated the flashlight. Lifting his phone, he swept the flashlight beam across the area. The intruder was gone. He'd slipped out of Sean's grasp, again.

Disconnecting the flashlight app, he shoved the phone into his pocket and made his way across the yard. Time to get back to Jenna. He'd make a sweep through the house first and make sure all the doors and windows were locked. Then he'd get Jenna to the safety of his house. Hopefully, she'd followed his directions and called for backup. The intruder was most likely long gone, but the officers would file a report and look around to see if he'd left any clues.

Sean climbed the steps to the back deck and entered the open door, stepping into the laundry room of Jenna's home. He automatically reached to flip on the light switch but caught himself. The electricity company had temporarily disconnected power to the house because of the fire damage.

"There's another flashlight in the drawer next to the refrigerator," Jenna yelled from the hallway.

He crossed to the drawer, opened it and felt around inside until his fingers brushed against the flashlight. Grasping it, he powered it on. "I thought I told you to go back to the truck."

"You did, but…" There was a grunt, followed by the

sound of something being dragged. "I wanted to see what the intruder was looking for."

He sprinted around the furniture and down the hall. Jenna shoved a box across the threshold of the first room on the right, pushing it in front of Sean. He jumped out of the way. "What are you doing?"

Jenna straightened and turned back to the room. "Becca never lived in this home. When I walked away from my job in education, I had to sell the home I raised my daughter in and downsize. But I couldn't bring myself to part with her furniture or any of her stuff, so I moved it here and put it in this room."

Sean scooted the box aside, stepped into the doorway and scanned the room with the flashlight's beam. She had decorated the walls with various pictures of herself and her daughter through the ages.

"As you can probably tell, I didn't decorate the room exactly the way Becca had left her old one, but I think you can admit it would be easy for anyone to tell that this furniture and these items belonged to a teenage girl."

The bed had a few stuffed animals resting on the pillows, and there was a jewelry box and several photos of Becca and her friends on the dresser. He nodded. "I would agree."

She sighed. "But what I haven't figured out is why the intruder was in this room. What was he searching for?"

"What do you mean? How do you know he was searching this room?" Sean swept his light around the room once more.

The dresser drawers appeared to be undisturbed, but the closet door stood wide open. Boxes of books and other memorabilia had been dumped on the floor. Several were open and tossed aside. "Did he do that?" Sean fixed the beam of light onto the pile of stuff.

"Yes." She crossed to the closet, settled onto the floor and started placing books back into the boxes.

"Whoa. Wait a minute." He put out a hand to halt her. "You shouldn't disturb a crime scene."

"Seriously?" She dropped the book she was holding into the box, then pushed to her feet. "Do you really think the police will get any clues from this?"

He wanted to say yes, but he couldn't. The only thing the scene before him proved was that the intruder had been inside this room. And as much as he wanted to argue that they might get fingerprints, he seriously doubted that would be the case. Even the most novice criminal knew to wear gloves when entering a home. "I don't know. But they should at least see it. They may want to take pictures."

Jenna plopped down onto the bed, and her shoulders slumped. He knelt on the floor beside her. "Did you call Heath like I asked?"

She nodded. Her long brown hair fell like a curtain, hiding her from his scrutiny. "He should be here soon. Said he'd come out himself."

Reaching out, Sean swept the hair back and tucked it behind her ear. "After Heath looks at the room, I'll help you get everything boxed up. We can take whatever you want back to my house. Okay?"

A lone tear slid out of the corner of her eye and down her cheek. He brushed it away with his thumb, and she captured his hand and pulled it away. Sean suddenly felt self-conscious about his actions. He'd only intended to offer support and hadn't meant to cross boundaries. "I… ah… I'm sorry."

She shook her head. "You have nothing to apologize for. I'm just—"

"Sean! Jenna! Where are y'all?" Heath yelled from the front of the house.

Sean shoved to his feet and stepped into the hall. "We're here."

Footsteps drew closer, and Heath stepped into the hall-way, a flashlight in his hand.

"The intruder got away. But we think he was searching for something in Becca's belongings." Sean moved to the side to allow the sheriff to enter the room.

Jenna remained seated but pointed to the pile of boxes and books dumped in and around the closet floor. "I looked through the rest of the house, but this seems to be the only room touched. Of course, I could have missed something." She shrugged. "It would be easier to tell if there was electricity."

"Well, since that isn't an option at the moment and—" Heath glanced at the box in the hall "—you apparently want to pack Becca's things, I suggest we go from room to room and take a quick look. With three flashlights, we should be able to get a pretty clear visual."

She nodded, stood and swept her hand toward the door. "Lead the way."

Twenty minutes later, they had searched every room of the house. None of the other rooms appeared to be disturbed.

Heath used his cell phone to snap photos of the boxes on the floor of the closet in the room that housed Becca's things. "It seems the intruder was looking for something specific." He turned to Jenna. "I really should load all this up and haul it to the station and have one of my deputies go through it to see if they can pick up on any clues."

"How would they know what they're looking at? They didn't know Becca, and—"

"Agreed. Also, as it has been pointed out many times, we're shorthanded. So…" Heath turned to Sean.

"So you're wondering if I'll be the lead detective—pro bono, of course." Sean raised an eyebrow.

"Hey, you know I'd put you on the payroll in half a heartbeat. All you have to do is say the word." Heath held out his hands, palms upward. "But since you don't want to come work for me, I'm asking you, as a friend, if you can help me decipher the clues in this case."

"You don't even have to ask. I already told Jenna that I'd help her box everything up and take it to my house. We can go through everything once we get it there." Sean glanced at her for verification, and she nodded. He turned to Heath. "If you'll help me, we can get these items loaded into my vehicle."

Sean picked up the box Jenna had shoved into the hall earlier and strode toward the front door. His heart raced as adrenaline surged through him. Why did it feel so good for his detective skills to be needed once again? He'd thought he was way past wanting to put his life on the line to protect civilians. Maybe being a protector wasn't something one ever got over. It was part of their DNA. He'd never intentionally gone out looking to put his life on the line, but solving cases and helping bring closure to loved ones was invigorating. Was that the same feeling Jenna felt when she used her podcast to help solve cold cases? Sure, her daughter's case had prompted her early foray into true crime podcasting—a form of investigative journalism in its own right—but being willing to put her life on the line, not just for her own daughter's unsolved murder but for other families seeking justice for their loved ones, was about more than a mother's love. Maybe he'd been wrong about her.

Jenna dropped the box she was carrying onto the big table that took up most of the space in the dining nook that sat in the corner of Sean's farmhouse kitchen. Sean and Heath trailed in behind her and sat their boxes beside hers. Five boxes in total, all containing Becca's high school memories. "Thanks, guys. I'm not sure what the intruder could have been looking for, but maybe there's something in here that will lead me to the killer."

"I think you mean *us*. Lead *us* to the killer. Remember, you're not in this alone, anymore." Sean dropped an arm across her shoulders, and a warm, protected feeling spread over her.

"That's right," Heath agreed. "You have us now. And I'm truly sorry I didn't look into Becca's death sooner. I should have gone over the file myself when I took office and not blindly accepted Sheriff Rice's assertion that it was suicide."

She turned to face her friend. It was nice to hear him admit he'd messed up, though she couldn't fault him for accepting his predecessor's assessment on cases the department had deemed closed. "Thank you. But we can't dwell on mistakes of the past. We have too much to keep us busy in the present. Learn from it and move on."

A smile spread across his face, and she could see hints

of the young boy she'd babysat all those years ago. "You're very gracious."

No. She wasn't. She was simply learning to let past hurts go so they wouldn't fester and spread like a disease and engulf her.

"Okay, I need to get going. I plan to go to the high school in the morning and interview the faculty and staff. See if anyone remembers anything they may not have thought was important four years ago." He searched her face. "I know it isn't standard practice to bring victims' families on these types of interviews, but I was wondering if you and Sean would meet me there. You know the faculty and staff better than I do, and you may be able to tell if they're hiding anything by their body language."

Slowly releasing a breath, she thought of all her coworkers and so-called friends who had faded from her life when she'd refused to give up on finding Becca's murderer. She hadn't faced any of them in two and a half years. Not since overhearing the conversation in the teacher's lounge the day she'd announced she was quitting so she could work full-time on Becca's case. Not one person supported her decision. They'd all thought she had taken a headfirst dive off the deep end. But that didn't matter now. With Sean and Heath beside her, she could confront the naysayers. "Sure. We'll be there."

"I'll text you in the morning to let you know what time I'll be there." He gave her a quick hug and then headed for the door. "Let me know if y'all find anything of interest in the boxes."

Stopping midway, he turned back to Sean. "Keep her safe. This guy is getting too close. I know you stayed in the camper last night to give her privacy and space, but you may need to sleep inside tonight."

"Agreed." Sean cast a quick glance in her direction, as if he expected her to argue.

Jenna pressed her lips together and stayed quiet. She didn't have any experience with evading killers, having only ever dealt with them from the other side of a microphone and a computer. There was no way she was about to tell these two lawmen how to do their job, especially when the task at hand was keeping her alive.

"Okay. I'll have one of my deputies drive by periodically throughout the night. I'll also have him check on your house in case the intruder goes back there tonight. And in the morning, we'll see about getting someone out there to secure your home a little better to keep him—or any other would-be vandals—out."

"I appreciate that. Tell whomever you call to send me a bill, and I'll see that they're paid quickly."

Heath tipped his head and slipped outside. Sean caught the door before it closed completely and whistled for Beau to come inside. After the coonhound had bounded into the room, Sean shut the door and locked the dead bolt.

Beau came and sat at Jenna's feet, and she bent down and scratched between his ears. "Were you so happy to get to run outside after being locked indoors all day? You're such a good boy."

One of the few regrets Jenna had as a mom was never getting a dog for Becca. She hadn't wanted the responsibility of having to care for anyone else besides herself and her daughter. And living in a condo that lacked a sizable fenced-in backyard meant a dog would have to stay locked inside for long hours each day. It hadn't seemed fair to the animal. So when Becca was eight and started begging for a dog like her friend Patty had, Jenna had listed all the reasons they couldn't own a dog and driven Becca to the pet store and allowed her to pick out an animal that could live in her tiny bedroom and didn't require long walks outdoors. Which was how they'd ended up with a guinea pig named Harry—a pet that was supposed to have had a life expectancy of five to seven years that ended up living nine, dying just two months after Becca had.

A tear slid down her cheek, and she quickly buried her face in Beau's fur. What would Sean think if she kept allowing her emotions to run unchecked? One of her biggest fears in life was appearing weak to others, a leftover emotion from her divorce. Patrick's last words to her as he walked out the door had been, "Run home to your mommy. You'll never make it on your own. You are a weak human being who needs to be taken care of. There's no way you'll be able to raise Becca alone."

And Jenna had done exactly as he'd said. She'd run home to Barton Creek and moved into her mother's house, but only for two years. Once she'd completed her teaching degree and gotten a job, she purchased a condo and started her new life as a single mom.

Sean cleared his throat. She pulled back from Beau and met Sean's gaze, a frown on his face, concern etched in his eyes. Had he seen the tear? *Please don't let him mention it if he did.*

He looked from her to the coonhound and back again. "I put a pizza in the oven. It should be ready in about twenty minutes. If you want to…um…go wash up or relax, I'll feed Beau. Then we can eat before we go through the boxes."

How had she missed him getting the pizza out of the freezer and putting it in the oven? She really needed to get a grip and stay aware of the things going on around her. Jenna had been so oblivious. Lost in her own emotions and thoughts, she'd completely tuned out her surroundings. That the killer could have snuck up on her if this had happened anywhere else made Jenna suddenly nauseated. She nodded. "Okay."

After giving Beau one last pat on the head, she turned and quickly made her way to the guest room. Once inside, she closed the door, crossed to the bed and lay down. If she could close her eyes for just a few minutes, maybe she would stop feeling like her world was spinning out of control.

Some time later, Jenna opened her eyes. Where was she? *Oh, yeah, Sean's house.* She swung her legs off the side of the bed, sat up and listened. The house was quiet. How long had she been asleep? She'd only intended to close her eyes for a few minutes.

What time was it? She didn't know how long she'd slept. It could have been a few minutes or a few hours. Fumbling with the lamp on the bedside table, she found the knob and twisted it. She blinked her eyes repeatedly until they adjusted to the light. Her phone wasn't on the nightstand. It must still be on the kitchen table. Pushing to her feet, she plodded across the carpeted floor and slowly opened the door. Why did she feel like an intruder? It might not even be that late. The kitchen light shone like a beacon in the distance. She headed in that direction.

"You're awake. Are you hungry?" Sean spoke from behind her.

A small scream escaped her lips, and she jumped, spinning around to face him. "You startled me," she accused, clutching her chest.

He reached out a hand and steadied her. "I'm sorry."

"What time is it?"

"Just after ten. You slept for about two hours."

"Why didn't you wake me when the pizza was done?"

"I thought about it but decided you needed sleep more than you needed food." He smiled. "But now that you're awake, how does cold pizza or a grilled cheese sandwich sound?"

Her stomach growled, and she giggled. "Actually, grilled cheese sandwiches are my favorite comfort food."

"Good. I also put on a pot of coffee earlier. It should still be hot." He gently turned her toward the kitchen and escorted her down the hall. "If you're afraid the caffeine will keep you awake the rest of the night, I can always make a fresh pot of decaf."

"Coffee sounds nice. Caffeinated is fine. Since I had such a long nap, it will be okay if I'm awake for a few hours."

They reached the kitchen, and she noticed he had shifted the boxes. There were stacks of Becca's things scattered all over the table.

"Here, I'll move this aside. We can—"

"No!" She reached out and halted him before he could push a stack of yearbooks aside. "I'll move them. I can't believe you touched Becca's things while I was asleep. Why would you do that?"

"Because I'm searching for her killer and trying to stop you from becoming his next victim," he stated in a calm, matter-of-fact tone. Then he stepped back, crossed to the refrigerator, and removed the cheese and butter.

Her cheeks warmed. She'd had no right to snap at him. He had saved her life four times in the past forty-eight hours and had even opened his home to her so she would be safe. "I'm… I'm sorry. I didn't mean…" Her voice cracked. She took a deep breath and released it slowly. "Did you find anything suspicious?"

He placed a pat of butter into a cast-iron skillet on the stove and watched it sizzle. Then he added the cheese sandwich into the hot skillet. "No. Nothing that jumped out at me as a clue," he replied after several long minutes. "I quickly realized—since I'd never met your daughter— that going through the boxes alone was a waste of time. That's why I was in my office reading and not in here looking for clues when you woke up."

She didn't have a right to probe into his private life, but curiosity got the better of her. "What were you reading?"

He flipped the sandwich in the skillet and reached into the cabinet and removed a plate. Then he turned off the stove, plated the sandwich and placed it on the kitchen table in front of her. She met his gaze. Maybe she should apologize for being nosy. She opened her mouth.

"The Bible," he said softly before she could speak.

Of all the answers he could have given, she wasn't sure why this one surprised her, but it did. Maybe because she hadn't made church or reading her Bible a priority since Becca died. The last time she'd even stepped inside the church building had been for Becca's funeral. Come to think of it, she didn't have a clue where her Bible was. She vaguely remembered packing it when she sold the condo but couldn't recall where she'd put it once she moved into her house. But she knew exactly where Becca's Bible was. She turned and looked at the boxes on the table. Sitting in front of the box labeled *Becca's Prized Belongings* was the red leather Bible with the name *Rebecca Lynn Hartley* stamped in gold lettering on the bottom-right corner.

"Finding your daughter's well-worn, well-loved Bible reminded me I hadn't spent enough time in mine in a while," Sean said from behind her, as if reading her thoughts.

Sadly, Jenna hadn't spent time in her Bible in a while, either. Almost four years. Though she wasn't proud to admit it.

TEN

Sean scrubbed a hand over his face, the stubble of his five-o'clock shadow scratching his palm. It was nearing midnight, and his eyes felt gritty, as if he'd walked through a sandstorm. He blinked several times, but it didn't help. Pushing his chair back, he crossed to the sink and splashed cold water on his face.

"If you want to go to bed, I'm fine working alone," Jenna said.

He turned to face her and leaned against the counter. They had looked at every memento and piece of paper in four of the boxes. Only one to go. He didn't know if it was best to keep pushing through or if he should encourage her to take a break so both of them could get some rest. Which would enable them to look at the items with fresh eyes tomorrow.

"I'd feel better if you got some sleep, too."

She reached into the last box and pulled out a school yearbook. "I'm not sleepy."

He went to stand behind the chair he'd vacated earlier. "I know you want to find answers tonight. But sometimes you have to know when to walk away for a little while. If you keep pushing yourself past the point of exhaustion, you're more likely to miss a valuable clue."

"Really, I'm fi—"

"I know." He gently tugged the yearbook out of her hand and placed it back in the box. "You're fine. But I'm not. And I won't be able to sleep as long as I know you're still up."

Her brown eyes searched his. Then she pressed her lips together and nodded. "I get it. Having a guest in your home disrupts your routine. You won't sleep as well if you're worried about hearing every sound I make anytime I move.

"I'll retire to the guest room so you can get some rest." She stood, and Beau was instantly by her side.

"Thank you." Sean clicked the button to turn on the range-hood light, something his mom did when guests visited her house. Once, when he was eight years old, he'd asked her why she always did that, and she'd told him it was so their guests wouldn't trip over the furniture in an unfamiliar home if they woke up in the middle of the night needing a glass of water. "Come on, Beau. Time for bed."

Jenna scratched the coonhound's head. "If you don't mind, can he stay with me? He slept beside my bed last night. It was comforting."

Beau looked up at him with pleading eyes, as if he knew they were discussing him. Sean liked routine, which meant Beau sleeping in the sunroom. But if the coonhound gave Jenna comfort, how could he say no? Though he was sure he'd have one sad dog on his hands when this ordeal was over and Jenna was no longer there to slip treats to Beau under the table or allow him to sleep with her.

"I guess I can move his bed into your room, for now. Try to get some rest, okay? Remember, we're meeting Heath at the school in the morning." Sean followed Jenna out of the room, snaking out his hand to turn off the overhead light as he passed the wall switch.

Beau let out a loud, drawn-out howl, and goosebumps prickled Sean's skin. Was someone outside?

A bullet shattered the window above the sink and struck the wall just above the light switch.

"Get down!" Sean yelled, and dropped to the floor, regretting his decision to leave the light on over the stove.

"Quickly, get into the hall," he commanded Jenna, who swiftly followed his instructions, crawling on her hands and knees.

Two more bullets came through the dining room window, one piercing the glass front of his grandmother's china cabinet and the other hitting the back of one of the dining chairs.

They reached the safety of the hallway, where there weren't any windows, and Jenna settled against the wall with her knees pulled to her chest and an arm wrapped around Beau—the coonhound barking and straining to get free.

"Beau. Quiet!" Sean commanded. The dog instantly stopped barking and sat, proving obedience training had been worth the time and expense.

"Now what?" Jenna asked.

"Do you have your phone?"

"Yes."

"Call this in. And stay here. I'm going to slip into my bedroom and retrieve my gun."

She reached into her back pocket and pulled out her cell while he headed for his bedroom at the end of the hall. The lights in this part of the house were all turned off, so he prayed the shooter wouldn't be able to follow his movements. The gunfire had stopped, and that made him very nervous. He needed his weapon, and he needed to make sure Jenna was somewhere safe so he could go outside and capture this guy.

Sean reached his bedside table, opened the drawer, pulled out his Glock and stuck it into the back of his waistband. Now, what about Jenna? He couldn't take her outside with him.

"Police are en route," she whispered from the doorway, Beau pressed against her side.

"Great. I have to go outside and try to stop this guy. The hall bathroom is an interior room without windows. I think you'll be safest there." What if the guy breached the house and found her hiding in there? She'd be trapped, and Beau would be no match against a gun. "Do you know how to shoot a rifle?"

"It's been years, but I'm sure I can manage."

Staying low, he went over to the closet and pulled out the .22 hunting rifle his grandfather had given him for his fifteenth birthday. "Be careful. It's loaded, and there's a live round in the chamber."

The bedroom window shattered, and a bullet whizzed past his head, hitting the closet door. Sean dove to the other side of the bed and slid the rifle toward Jenna. "Get into the bathroom. Now!" He propped his arms on the bed and returned fire, thankful she had followed instructions and not insisted on sticking around and helping.

Sean and the assailant exchanged several rounds of bullets. Then the sound of a police siren pierced the night. The shots from outside halted. Convinced the shooter had taken off, Sean pushed to his feet. "You can come out now. He's gone."

Jenna rushed into the room. "Are you okay?"

"Yeah. I'm fine." He looked around his bedroom. Two walls were peppered with holes and would need to be patched, but in the grand scheme of things, that was a minor issue. He was thankful no one had been injured. "Where's Beau?"

"I put him in the guestroom so he'd be out of the way."

"Good thinking."

There was a loud banging on the front door. "Everyone okay in there?"

"That sounds like Deputy Moore." Sean led the way back to the front of the house and opened the door to allow the uniformed officer inside. "We're fine. The shooter took off when he heard the sirens."

"My partner is following him through the woods. But he had a big head start, so I wouldn't hold out too much hope that he's captured tonight." Deputy Moore's phone rang, and he glanced at the screen. "Excuse me. I'll take this outside."

Sean glanced at Jenna, noticing her pale complexion and trembling hands for the first time. Was she going into shock? "I think you and I should wait in the living room."

He slipped his arm around her shoulders and guided her through the open doorway. Once inside, he directed her to sit on the couch. Then he snagged the thick redplaid throw off the ottoman in front of the fireplace and draped it across her shoulders. "Give me a few minutes, and I can have a fire started."

"There's no need for that. I'm fine. The blanket will be enough." She smiled up at him, her lower lip trembling.

That was his undoing. He instantly settled onto the couch next to her, put his arm around her and pulled her into a warm embrace. All he could think of was that he needed to reassure her that he was there to protect her and everything would be okay. He would do whatever it took to keep from seeing that look of sheer helplessness in her eyes ever again.

The front door opened, and Sean scooted several inches away from Jenna as if he were a teenage boy who'd just been caught kissing. He stood as Deputy Moore entered the room.

The deputy held out his phone to Sean. "Sheriff Dalton wishes to speak with you."

Sean accepted the phone and tapped the screen to place the call on speaker. Otherwise, he'd just have to repeat everything to Jenna. "Hi, Heath. I've placed you on speaker. Jenna's here, too."

"Good. Are you both okay?"

"We're fine," they said in unison.

"I'm guessing I wouldn't be able to convince you to move to a different location, would I?"

Sean looked at Jenna, though he knew her answer before he did. She shook her head vigorously. "Becca's things are here. We'd have to move all the boxes, and my laptop and belongings."

"I can have—"

"We appreciate the offer, but she's right. We can't leave all those things here, and it would be too much trouble to move it all tonight." He rubbed the back of his neck. "We'll be okay. I won't let him get the jump on us again."

A sigh sounded across the line. "I believe you two are equally matched in stubbornness. Okay, but I'll have my men stay. They can stand guard outside overnight so both of you can get some rest. You've had a long day, being shot at twice."

"There's no need for that," Sean protested.

"There is. And you won't argue, or I'll have my men take you into the station for questioning."

"But—"

"You know I can do it," came the stern reply.

Jenna clutched Sean's arm, and he met her pleading gaze. He puffed out a breath. "Fine. Thank you."

"Don't mention it. Just keep Jenna safe. And get some rest. Hopefully, tomorrow we can find a new lead."

Sean handed the phone back to Deputy Moore just as his partner entered the house. The deputy—who introduced himself as Deputy Bishop—said the intruder had cut through the woods to an old, overgrown logging road that was midway between Sean's and Jenna's houses. Then he'd jumped into a pickup truck and taken off before Deputy Bishop could get close enough to identify the make or model, or get a tag number.

"Will anyone ever be able to stop this guy?" Jenna demanded.

"We're sure going to try, ma'am," Deputy Moore replied before Sean could. "In the meantime, try to get some rest. I doubt he'll return tonight, but if he does, we'll be waiting for him."

"Thank you." Sean showed the men out and bolted the door behind them, a strange sensation settling in the pit of his stomach. He was used to being the one doing the guarding, not the one being guarded. The feeling of needing others to help him do the job he'd been assigned to do was not one he enjoyed. Whatever it took, Sean *would* protect Jenna.

ELEVEN

Jenna chewed her lower lip. She hadn't seen any of her former coworkers, except in passing, since she'd walked away from her job. The eighteen months she worked after Becca's death had been awkward, and her relationships with both the faculty and the students had been strained. Meeting people's eyes and seeing pity etched in them had made her self-conscious. She would walk up to a group of teachers, and they'd stop talking. Students she'd worked hard to build trust with had stopped coming to her for guidance. When she'd questioned the behaviors, her principal had told her to give it time. He'd said it would only be natural for the students to be hesitant to talk to her about their college plans and their futures when they thought hearing such things would be painful for her, knowing her daughter would experience none of the things they were about to do.

"You're going to make your lips bleed if you don't stop worrying," Sean said, breaking into her thoughts. "If you're this worried about going to the school, I can always drop you off at the sheriff's office."

"No. I'd rather stay with you. Besides, Heath is right. I know these people better than both of you do. They may not be open to discussing things they remember, but I should be able to tell if they're covering up something. You don't work with people for ten years without learning how to read them."

"If you're sure."

"I'm sure."

They rode in silence until they turned into the school parking lot fifteen minutes later. Sean parked beside Heath's green-and-white sheriff's department SUV.

"Let's do this." Jenna opened her door and stepped out, pulling her coat tighter to ward off the stiff wind that ruffled her hair. "Brr."

Sean rounded the vehicle, placed a hand on her lower back and hurried her to the main entrance of the building.

Heath met them in the foyer. "I'm glad y'all could come. Today is a teacher workday. There won't be many students on campus other than the football team and the band students who are having practices."

"That's probably for the best. We wouldn't want to interrupt classes, anyway." Jenna shrugged out of her coat and draped it across her arm. "This year's senior class would have been in middle school when Becca died. I doubt they'd offer much insight into her death."

They made their way to the office where Principal Fisher and the school counselor, Mrs. Hill, waited for them with the school resource officer, Deputy Manning. Jenna greeted each of them. Mrs. Hill, who'd been Jenna's mentor her first year teaching, pulled her into a warm, motherly hug, and some of Jenna's apprehension evaporated. The people at the school were her work family. They had meant nothing when they questioned her ability to do her job after Becca's passing, and if they'd seemed awkward around her, it was only because they were concerned about her and didn't know how to help her through the pain.

"It's so good to see you," Mrs. Hill whispered in her ear.

"I've missed you," Jenna replied, hugging her friend tighter.

They pulled apart, both with tears glistening in their eyes.

"I have asked Officer Manning to escort you today. We have notified the staff that you're on campus and wish to interview them." Principal Fisher pinned Jenna with a stern gaze. "While I'm not sure what you hope to accomplish here today, everyone has agreed to be cooperative and answer all of your questions. Even the ones they've answered before. Multiple times. We all want you to get the closure you are searching for."

Jenna felt Sean stiffen beside her. But she pressed her lips together and nodded. Principal Fisher wasn't known for his tact. He hated when things disrupted his schedule. Quite honestly, he probably would have been better suited to just about any other job than that of a high school principal, which actually required a great deal of flexibility with schedules and routines.

"I appreciate everyone's understanding. Especially since I've reopened the case and plan to do a full investigation myself," Heath said, his tone making it clear he wouldn't tolerate any more snide comments.

Principal Fisher bristled. "I'll be in my office. *If* you need me." He turned and walked away.

Heath and Sean exchanged smiles as if they'd just stopped the schoolyard bully from stealing her lunch money.

Thank You, Lord, for placing people in my life who

stand with me and want to solve Becca's murder. Prayer seemed to be getting easier for her. Maybe she'd read in Becca's Bible when she got back to Sean's house.

"If you all will follow me, we'll start in the freshman hall. From there, we'll make our way to the senior hall before looping back through the sophomore and junior halls." Officer Manning led them out of the office.

An hour and a half later, they had spoken to every faculty member except the football coach and his staff. Officer Manning walked them to the football field, stopping just outside the gate. "I'm going to leave you here. I need to get back to the office and make some calls concerning truancy." He glanced at his watch. "Practice is scheduled to be over at noon, so it looks like you have about a fifteen-minute wait. In the meantime, you can sit on the bleachers and watch the team scrimmage. Then Coach Kent will meet you in his office in the field house."

"I need to make a quick phone call. I'll be right back." Heath pulled out his phone and went to stand by the chain-link fence that encircled the field.

Sean swept his hand toward the cold metal bleachers. "Ladies first."

Jenna bounded up the stairs, her footsteps thumping on the metal steps. Reaching the landing, she paused. Coach Kent's son, Tristan, sat on the top row of the bleachers watching the practice. She hadn't expected to see him here. The university was only a few hours from Barton Creek, but still she would have expected the starting quarterback—and projected first-round draft pick—to be on campus, attending classes and finishing up his coursework. After all, graduation was only a few months away.

She started to sit in the closest row, but Sean placed a hand on her shoulder, stopping her.

"Who's the guy at the top?" he asked in a hushed tone.

"Tristan Kent, the coach's son."

"Let's go sit by him. Maybe we can question him."

"It would be a waste of time."

"Why do you say that?"

"For starters, he was a year ahead of Becca, so he was already away at college when she was murdered."

"Doesn't mean he couldn't have heard something when he came home that might lead us to the killer. Did he and Becca have any classes together when he was still in high school? Or maybe have some friends in common?"

"I believe they had a literature class together Becca's sophomore year, and they may have had a math class together her junior year. As far as having friends in common, I don't remember her ever talking about him. I would think, if they attended the same parties and things, she might have mentioned him."

"Let's go to the top."

She glared at him. Wasn't he listening to her?

"I know you think it's a waste of time. But sometimes the people you think know nothing are the best kinds of witnesses. They see or hear things they don't even realize are important, and then they freely share that information. Besides, we have to sit somewhere, so why not near him?" He turned and headed up the bleachers, taking the stairs two at a time.

Jenna went after him. If nothing else, it would be nice to speak to a former student who was doing so well and on a clear path to work in his chosen profession.

As they neared the top row, Tristan stood. "Ms. Hartley. How are you? I didn't expect to see you at Dad's practice."

"I could say the same for you, Tristan." She gave him a sideways hug. "It's good to see you, but I'm surprised you're here in the middle of a semester."

A frown marred the handsome young man's face, and he shrugged one shoulder. "Something came up at home. I'm only here for a quick visit."

"Well, I'm glad I saw you. You're the hometown hero. We'll all be glued to our televisions watching the football draft, cheering for you."

"I'm not a hero, but thank you for your kind words." He looked out over the field. "Looks like Dad just finished up practice. I've gotta go meet him in the locker room."

Tristan made a move to go around her, but Sean stepped into his path. "If you could spare a moment, I wanted to ask you about Becca's murder."

Shock registered on the young man's face. "Why would you ask me about that? I wasn't in high school then."

"I know, but you may have heard someone talk about it. Anything at all. No matter how small you think it may be."

"I don't know what to tell you." Tristan turned to Jenna. "Other than I am sorry…for your loss."

"It's okay, Tristan. I know you and Becca didn't hang out with the same group of friends. So I didn't really expect you to have any information on her death." She forced a smile. "Go on. Tell your dad we had to leave, but we may want to talk to him later."

"Yes, ma'am." He jogged down the steps and ran toward the field house.

"Why did you tell him we'd talk to his dad later? Why not talk to him now since we're here?"

"Coach Kent didn't even know Becca. She wasn't a cheerleader, never attended the games and never had him for a teacher." Jenna sighed. "I have a headache, *and* I'm ready to go. Please." She stepped around him and ambled down the same steps Tristan had just taken. The interaction with the young man had been awkward. For the first time since Becca's death, Jenna felt uncomfortable probing for answers. What right did they have putting innocent people—people who had only known Becca in passing, if at all—on the spot like that?

They reached the bottom step when a frightening idea popped into her head. Jenna spun around to face Sean and lost her footing. His arm snaked out. He caught her and pulled her against him, preventing her from tumbling onto the asphalt track that surrounded the football field.

Her breath caught. Was that his heartbeat or her own echoing in her ear? Muffled words swirled in a fog around her. She pressed her eyes closed and counted to three. Then she pressed her hands against his rock-solid chest and pushed free of his hold.

"Thank you. Um. I'm not normally so clumsy."

"What happened? You spun around so fast…"

The crease in his brow deepened as he studied her, and she fought the urge to squirm.

"It's just… It suddenly occurred to me we could put innocent people in danger by going around asking questions. If the killer sees us talking to someone and he thinks they know more than they do, he could go after them." She wrapped her arms around her waist and hugged herself tightly. Jenna would not be able to forgive herself if she ever were the reason another family had to say goodbye to a loved one.

* * *

Sean narrowed his eyes and assessed the woman in front of him. She looked like she might collapse at any moment. He wrapped an arm around her shoulders and headed toward the exit.

Heath came up to them. "Was that Tristan Kent I saw you talking to? Hey, where are you going? We haven't spoken to Coach Kent and his staff yet."

"*We're* headed back to my house," Sean replied without breaking stride. "Jenna's had enough for one day. And no one today could offer any new information. So maybe it's time to take a step back, regroup and assess how to proceed."

Heath walked with them, looking from Jenna to Sean and back again. "That sounds like a good idea. I'll go talk to Coach Kent since I'm already here. But I'll check in with you later. Also, I'm assigning two deputies to watch your house again tonight—"

Jenna stopped in her tracks. "I thought the reason I was staying at Sean's was because you didn't have the personnel to assign deputies to watch me. That he was supposed to protect me."

"Yes, but the shooter got too close last night. So I—"

"And *Sean* protected me. Like he said he would," she replied, in a tone that brooked no argument.

Her fierce defense of him caught Sean by surprise. He wasn't sure if he should be flattered or annoyed. Did she think he needed defending?

Sean pulled back and looked at Jenna. Her face was flushed, and her eyes shone. She'd never looked more beautiful. *Whoa. Where'd that thought come from?* "Look, I—"

"No one said he didn't protect you," Heath said sternly.

"If I thought you weren't being protected, I *would* assign officers to guard you twenty-four hours a day. As it is, I'm just sending help for the overnight shift. So you *and* Sean can get some rest knowing someone else is standing watch."

Jenna's mouth formed an O.

Heath's face softened, and he pulled Jenna into an embrace. Sean's gut tightened. He gave himself a mental shake. It wasn't any of his business if the sheriff hugged Jenna. Besides, Heath was at least ten years younger than her. And hadn't she said she used to babysit him when he was a child?

The embrace ended, and Heath met Sean's gaze, one eyebrow arched quizzically. "I'll escort y'all to your vehicle. Take her back to your place. And I'll have my officers out there by nightfall."

Sean hated he couldn't just say no to his friend, but Heath made sense. Sean couldn't protect Jenna if he wasn't rested. Although he knew, even with an officer outside standing watch, he wouldn't get more than a few hours of sleep, it would still be better than no sleep at all. "Thanks, buddy."

A little while later, Sean merged into traffic and headed out of town. "Do you want to tell me what happened back there? Why did you suddenly care if we had officers standing guard again tonight?"

"You said yourself when you volunteered to protect me that the police force was too small for Heath to assign an officer to look out for me. Why, then, would I want the night shift officers to be stuck guarding me? What if something happened in another part of the county that required their attention? It could be a matter of life or death, and they would be delayed because they were babysitting me overnight."

Her behavior was making sense. "Are you still concerned that the killer may have been around today and seen us questioning people on the school campus?"

"Of course I am." She twisted in her seat to look at him. "You're the one that told me when you first moved here that I was putting innocent people in danger with my actions. Yet today, you didn't seem to be concerned if innocent bystanders were being put in harm's way."

A muscle twitching in his jaw. *Choose your words carefully. She is hurt and scared.* "I never should've said that. And I believe I've already apologized for it, so I won't apologize again. But this is a little different. Our actions today were not reckless. Even if the killer saw us on campus today—which, by the way, would mean somewhere in your subconscious, you believe the killer is a member of the school faculty or staff—"

"I never said that. Nor do I believe it."

"Then why would you believe the killer saw us there today? Did you see anyone who didn't belong there on campus while we were walking around?"

She shook her head. "No. I recognized everyone we saw, and they were all employees of the school, except for Tristan."

"Do you think he could be the killer?"

"No."

"Okay, no one should be in danger because they spoke to us. If they were, then the killer we're seeking is one of your former coworkers. And he'd have to have reason to believe someone else knows his secret. If the killer thought anyone could identify him, do you really think that the person would be alive to talk to us?"

She settled back into her seat and turned to watch the scenery go by. He hated being short with her, but he needed her to understand that if Becca's killer did kill someone else, it wouldn't be her fault. *Just like it wasn't her fault the killer was after her.* If Sheriff Rice hadn't decided it was easier to label Becca's death a suicide than to admit he didn't know how to solve the case, Jenna wouldn't have started her podcast. She had only been doing what any good mother would do—fighting for justice for her child. No one would intentionally step into a killer's path, and Sean knew that. So why had he been so harsh with her in the beginning?

No changing it now. All he could do was protect her and help her find the answers she needed.

"We didn't finish going through that last box of Becca's things. Do you feel like tackling that when we get back to my house?"

"Sure," she replied, without looking in his direction.

Dear Lord, please don't let her get swallowed up by her pain and despair. I can't solve this case without her, and I can't protect her if I can't figure out who I'm protecting her from. I know the answer to Becca's murder is somewhere close by. Let me—no, let us—find it soon. And, Lord, please don't let Jenna's fear of an innocent person becoming this killer's next victim because of our investigation become a reality. If that were to happen, I don't know how she would overcome her grief and guilt.

Picking up the blue snowman mug Sean had placed in front of her some time ago, Jenna took a sip of coffee. And almost immediately spit it out again. *Yuck.*

"Do you want me to freshen it up?" Sean asked.

"What?" She frowned at him.

"Your coffee." He nodded at her mug. "It's cold, right? Which isn't surprising, since I fixed it for you an hour ago."

"Really? I didn't think it had been that long." She straightened and rubbed the back of her neck. "Okay, so yeah, I guess I lost track of time."

Jenna picked up her mug, pushed her chair back from the table, stood, crossed to the sink and dumped the contents down the drain. "I'm sorry I wasted the coffee."

"Don't be. I assure you, I've wasted my fair share of coffee through the years. When you're a detective working on a big case, there are a lot of cold cups of coffee involved." He shrugged. "Some you pour down the drain and some you drink because you've not stopped long enough to eat or drink anything else all day."

She looked out the window above the sink. The sun was setting over the Appalachian Mountains. Streaks of purple, gold, red and orange decorated the sky, like paint strokes on a canvas. It was a breathtaking view. One she had often enjoyed from the swing in the backyard of her condo, but one she hadn't taken the time to enjoy since moving into her current house.

Sean came over to stand beside her. "You seem deep in thought."

"Just admiring God's artwork." Her throat tightened, and she swallowed. "I'm ashamed to admit it, but I've not really given my relationship with Him much thought since I lost Becca."

"No need to be ashamed. I understand, probably more than you know. After Felicia died, I spent the next two years in a fog. It wasn't until I moved to Barton Creek that I found my way back to church and rekindled my relationship with the Lord." He leaned over to peer out the window. "I'm thankful to Heath for encouraging me to put in the effort. Of course, I still falter and struggle from time to time, when I let my grief overwhelm me. But I now realize my anger was misplaced. God wasn't the one who took Felicia away from me. Instead of *me* being the one that needed to forgive Him, *He* was the one who had to forgive me. One great thing about our Heavenly Father, He never stops loving us or welcoming us back into the fold."

His words settled over her. Mom and Amber had said similar words to her in the past, and it had always irritated her that they were *pushing* her to *forgive* God. Although she knew their words came from a place of love, somehow she'd always taken it as them being preachy. However, Sean's words hadn't come across that way. Was it because he'd suffered a similar loss? Maybe she should take Becca's Bible to bed with her tonight and reacquaint herself with the Word.

Sean went to the refrigerator, pulled out creamer and turned to her. "Would you like a fresh cup?"

"Yes. Thank you." She handed her mug to him.

He added a splash of creamer to their mugs and then poured hot black coffee into both of them. She accepted hers and returned to her chair at the table.

"I thought you drank your coffee black." Jenna took a sip of the hot liquid.

"Most of the time, but occasionally, I'll add creamer. Sometimes I'll even add a spoonful of sugar."

Jenna giggled. She had no idea why she thought what

he'd said was funny. Maybe the mental exhaustion of the past few days had caught up with her.

Sean's phone dinged. He picked it up and read a text message. "It's from Heath. The deputies standing watch tonight will be here within the hour. And he wants you to know that a couple of off-duty officers have volunteered to be on call and will tend to any issues in the county overnight." He smiled and quickly typed out a response. "Heath's mom is sending over beef stew and cornbread for our supper."

Jenna hated that Marilyn Dalton had gone to so much trouble, but she knew better than to refuse the kindness. "Send my thanks, too, please."

"Already done." He placed the phone back on the table and settled into the chair he'd vacated earlier. "Do you need a break? Or should we keep working until the food arrives?"

"I'm fine. Let's keep going."

There was only one more item they hadn't looked through yet, and that was Becca's senior yearbook. They had been handed out at school two days after Becca's death, so Becca had never even seen it.

Jenna pulled the yearbook out of the box and ran her hand over the cover. Instead of having Becca's teachers and classmates simply sign their name in a guest book to denote their attendance at Becca's funeral, Jenna had requested that they sign Becca's yearbook, leaving comments of memories they'd shared throughout her high school years. She gasped. "This…this triggered the attacks."

Jenna locked gazes with Sean. "I always record my podcasts five days before I upload them online so I have plenty of time to complete edits. As you know, in addition to the traditional audio version, I also post a video version of me recording the podcast. That way people can choose the format they prefer. At the end of the video version, I display a few inspirational quotes or something as a bonus for the people who choose to watch. When I edited last week's video, it was about ten minutes shorter than usual. Since there was a larger gap of time that needed to be filled, I pulled out this yearbook and shared some of the sweet comments Becca's classmates had written."

She jumped out of her chair. "I'll be right back."

Running through the house, she darted into the guest room, grabbed her laptop bag and raced back to the kitchen. Breathing hard, she plopped onto the chair, settled her laptop onto the table and powered it on. "I took snapshots of the quotes, being careful not to include the names of the authors since I didn't want to infringe upon anyone's privacy, and did a slideshow for the end of the podcast."

Sean scooted his chair closer and leaned in so he could see the laptop screen. "Who wrote the messages you displayed?"

"I don't remember." *Ugh.* If only she'd kept better records and written the names and quotes in one of her notebooks instead of just putting the pictures into a slideshow. "I took the pictures of the messages months ago. I was just saving them until I needed them."

She opened the folder for the podcast from last week and quickly fast-forwarded to the end. The first slide flashed on the screen. Becca, thanks for tutoring me through geometry. It was quickly replaced by another. I will never forget how you were always so kind to everyone. And another. You will forever be missed!

"How many are there?"

Jenna furrowed her brow. "I'm not sure. Maybe fifteen or sixteen. I just kind of threw some random ones in until I thought I had enough."

"Okay, so I guess we need to freeze the screen on each image and then look through the yearbook for the handwriting and wording that matches it."

She reached for a pen and paper. "Or, since this isn't really a two-person job, I can do this while you do something else."

He looked like he might argue, but then he nodded. "I'll feed Beau."

Jenna nodded and opened the yearbook. Her eyes scanned the pages, and she quickly located the first two quotes. After jotting down the quotes and the names of the students who'd written them, she excitedly turned the pages. It didn't surprise her that Becca's closest friends— her childhood friends—had written the first four quotes. Working her way through the book, she located all but one quote. Then, on the inside of the back cover, she spotted it, written in small cursive handwriting with sharp edges. *I will miss your laughter and your smile.*

Whose signature was that? She leaned in and squinted. *Tristan Kent.* Jenna collapsed against the chair. Did Tristan know Becca better than she thought? No. Maybe? Jenna's mind whirled. She pinched the bridge of her nose and squeezed her eyes shut.

"Do you have a headache?" Sean asked from behind her. "Should I get you some pain meds?"

"No." Jenna opened her eyes, looked up at him and shrugged. "I found all of the quotes I shared on the podcast. And I know who wrote them."

Sean rested his hip against the countertop and waited.

She swallowed. "One of them was written by Tristan Kent."

"And the rest of the quotes?"

Picking up the notepad, she held it out for him to inspect. "I've listed all the names."

"Tomorrow, we'll see how many of these people we can locate and question. After we finish, if we still have questions, we'll pay Tristan a visit."

"Do you think he knows more than he let on today?"

"I'm not a mind reader. I'm a detective." Sean frowned. "When we saw him today, Tristan said he didn't know anything. Before we question him again, we need evidence that he is lying. Otherwise, we're not going to get anywhere, and he's going to say we're badgering him and trying to frame him."

Jenna gasped. "I would never do that. And I do not believe Tristan Kent is a killer."

The thought that someone so young could kill and cover it up for so long was terrifying. No. She had to be right about Tristan. Her judgment couldn't be that bad.

TWELVE

Sean opened the front door and stepped out into the cold, bright morning. A crust of frost covered the grassy areas, and the sun glimmered off the ice crystals, making them sparkle like diamonds. The weather the past week had been cooler than normal. But he didn't mind. There was something invigorating about the fresh mountain air on a chilly February day.

A sheriff's department cruiser was parked to the side of the driveway, an officer sitting in the driver's seat, his attention focused on his computer. Sean puffed out a breath and watched as a small fog wafted into the air. Then he headed across the lawn with Beau at his heels. As he approached the cruiser, the driver-side door opened and Deputy Moore climbed out.

Sean held up the thermos of coffee and two disposable coffee cups he was carrying in his hands. "I thought you guys might like to have something to warm you up."

"Thank you." Deputy Moore accepted the thermos. "Chris is doing one last sweep of the perimeter. I'm sure he will appreciate this when he returns."

"Were there any disturbances overnight?"

"No. Everything was quiet. Almost eerily so."

Sean tilted his head. "What do you mean?"

"I'm sure it was nothing. But there were no sounds. All night. Not even movement or night noises of wildlife." The younger man shrugged. "Maybe it was too cold last night, and all the deer and raccoons and things found places to burrow and stay warm."

Sean pondered this. The deputy was probably correct in his assumption, but in all the nights he'd spent on this farm, he'd never known there to be complete silence. But now that he thought back to the evening before, he realized Beau hadn't barked once. And the coonhound always barked when he heard the raccoons and the foxes yapping in the night.

A chilly breeze blew through the trees, and he shivered. "Breakfast will be ready in ten minutes. We'd like it if you both joined us."

"Thank you, but we need to head on back to the station. We still have paperwork to complete and reports to file before we can go home to our families."

Sean understood all too well the desire to get home to a family but having to complete paperwork first, even on nights when there was no action. "Okay. Thank you for being the watchmen last night so I could get some shut-eye."

He tipped his head, then turned and jogged back to the house, lifting his hand to wave at the other deputy in passing.

Pounding through the front door, he inhaled deeply. The smell of sausage frying mixed with the scent of strong coffee, along with the sound of a woman humming as she worked, greeted him. He picked up his pace, joy in his heart. Rounding the corner to the dining room, his steps faltered, and he stopped, staring in disbelief. Jenna stood at the sink, looking out the window. The scene before him brought him crashing back to reality. Felicia was dead. Jenna had been the one humming. Though logically he'd known that when he heard the sound, his heart had momentarily forgotten.

Jenna turned and smiled at him, and his breath caught in his throat.

"Good morning," she greeted him in a singsongy voice.

He frowned. Why was she suddenly so chipper? The smile on her face faded away, and remorse settled over him. Sean cleared his throat. "Good morning. I take it you slept well?"

"Yes. I hope you did as well."

He nodded, unable to tell her yes but also unable to say no. While he had only slept about five hours, he had rested well.

"Will the officers be joining us for breakfast? I was about to scramble the eggs."

"I invited them, but they have to get back to the station." He crossed over to the refrigerator, opened it and removed the carton of eggs. She held out her hand, and he relinquished them to her. No point in arguing over who would cook the eggs, though he had never shared cooking duties with anyone other than Felicia. Even his grandmother had never allowed him in her kitchen—*this* kitchen—when she'd been alive.

"Are you going to tell me what put you in such a good mood?"

She broke an egg and emptied its contents into a bowl and whisked. "I'm not sure how to explain it, but I just feel like we're getting close to a breakthrough. That sounds silly, doesn't it? Considering I don't have any hard evidence to support the idea. But for the moment, I choose to embrace contentment and hope."

He settled at the table and picked up the notebook from the night before. "Are you still convinced Tristan Kent knows nothing about Becca's death?"

She poured the egg mixture into a sizzling-hot skillet, moving the golden liquid around with a spatula. He wondered if she was going to ignore his question as she removed shredded cheese from the refrigerator and added a generous sprinkle to the eggs.

"I know you think I'm being naive or that I'm not considering all options, but I really don't believe Tristan would kill anyone. I know him. He's a good kid." She reached into the cabinet and removed two plates. "A lot of boys would have broken under the pressure that he had to endure growing up. His dad pushed him every step of the way to be the best he could be at football. But Tristan loves his dad and only wants to make him proud."

Jenna plated the eggs, then placed one dish in front of him and the other at her seat. *Whoa*. When had he started thinking of that seat as Jenna's spot? He shoved a bite of egg into his mouth, chewed and swallowed, forcing the food past the lump lodged in his throat.

"He also has a cousin who has special needs," Jenna continued, obviously oblivious to Sean's inner struggle. "I have seen him stand up for her when others wanted to bully and make fun of her. I've also seen him carry books for an underclassman with a broken leg without being asked to do so. A lot of athletes who are viewed as superstars and are almost idolized by their classmates would have acted differently, maybe even joining in on the bullying. They would act tough and above the rules because they would want to fit in with their peers, but not Tristan. He always stood up for his beliefs."

She sat down and seasoned her eggs. "Does that sound like a kid who is a murderer?"

"Killers don't always fit a set stereotype. Several killers throughout history were seemingly good people."

A frown briefly marred her face. She forked a bite of egg and shoved it into her mouth.

There was nothing else to say, so they ate their meal in silence. When they finished, Sean stood and took both plates to the sink. "You cooked, so I'll do the cleanup."

"Sounds good." She drank the last of her coffee and then pushed back her chair. "If you'll excuse me, I need to go to my—the guest room—and work on my podcast."

"Before you go…" He scraped the remnants of the meal into the garbage disposal. "Why do you think Tristan came back for the funeral of an acquaintance? You said he was away at college when Becca died, right?"

"Yes, but it's only two hours away. So it's easy for him to make a quick trip home to Barton Creek, especially when football season is over."

"Do you still think they weren't friends?"

"I have no reason to believe they were more than acquaintances."

"Then explain to me why he would write what he did in her yearbook."

"Because he was in my Algebra I class his freshman year. He was a star student. And when I accepted the counselor's position his junior year, he made a point of telling me he thought I'd be great at the job, and he thanked me for preparing him for college. A kid who has a teacher they feel pushes them to be their best and helps them get into college would want to come and offer condolences at the death of that teacher's child. Besides, several people wrote in Becca's yearbook that they would miss her smile or miss her laughter. She was a joyful person, and people noticed. His comment could simply be a sign of respect."

He placed the last dish into the draining rack. "So do you think the person responsible for Becca's death is one of the other students?"

She offered a half shrug. "I don't know. I'll have to examine that more closely after I finish the edits on my show so I can schedule the upload. It's supposed to go live tomorrow."

"Are you sure that's a good idea?"

"What do you mean?"

"Just that right now, someone is desperately trying to kill you. Is it a good idea to post more content that might enrage him further?"

She raised an eyebrow. "Do you really think if I stopped the podcast today and never posted another episode, never spoke about Becca's death again, that it would make a difference, and the person who is after me would just go away?"

She had him there. He knew as well as she did that it didn't matter at this point what she said or did. The threat would not go away. He clenched his teeth, and his jaw muscle twitched.

"I didn't think so." She turned and walked out of the room without another word.

Lord, I hope she's right about Tristan. She defends him as if he were her own child. It's obvious she developed a strong bond with him when he was her student. I'd hate for her to discover he was involved in this.

Ten minutes later, he dried the last dish and placed it on

the shelf where it belonged. Then he turned off the light and headed down the hall toward his office. Pausing outside Jenna's door, he lifted a hand to knock and froze. He owed her an apology for arguing with her over petty issues. But he hated to interrupt her while she was working.

Entering his office, he went over to his desk and picked up his worn leather Bible, then settled into the oversize chair in the corner of the room. Opening the book, he started reading in Ecclesiastes, chapter three, where he'd left off last time.

Sean's phone rang, and he glanced at the ID. Douglas Anthony. Swiping his finger across the screen, he answered and put the phone on speaker. "Hello?"

"Sean. I hate to bother you, but a tree fell on my fence on the south side of the pasture, where our properties join. The missus and I leave tomorrow to visit her folks in Iowa, and I have to get it repaired today. But my ranch hand is in Nashville and won't be back until late this evening, so I don't have any help. Could you give me about an hour of your time? It's really a two-man job."

"Of cour—" He swallowed his reply. He couldn't leave Jenna. Could he convince her to put on a pair of his overalls and lend a hand? "Actually, Douglas, I'm not sure I can. I'm kind of in the middle of something here."

"What are you in the middle of?" Jenna stood in the doorway.

He pressed the mute button on his phone. "You know very well what I'm in the middle of. I can't just leave you here. Unless… Do you want to go out in the cold and help repair a barbed wire fence?"

"I would, but unfortunately, I have to finish my edits. That doesn't mean you can't go."

"I can't *leave you* here," he repeated.

She nodded at the phone in his hand.

"Sean? Sean, are you still there?" Douglas asked, over and over.

So distracted by the conversation with Jenna, Sean had completely tuned out the man on the phone.

He unmuted the device and took a deep breath. "I'm here. Sorry, but I'll get back to you. I won't be long."

After disconnecting the call, he turned his attention to Jenna. She stood with her hand on her hip. He had seen that same stance several times during his marriage, when his wife's opinions had differed from his. No matter. He would not give in to Jenna. Either they both went or neither did.

"Can you take your laptop and work in my vehicle while I help Mr. Anthony?"

"Not really." She relaxed her arms and leaned against the doorframe. "I appreciate that you're trying to keep me safe, but trying to work, sitting in a vehicle, while you and Douglas use a chain saw would be too distracting. He said it would take less than an hour, which means it's probably not a large tree. I can stay here, with all the doors and windows locked. Beau will be here to protect me, and I know where the rifle is if I need it."

"I'm st—"

"And," she said, interrupting his argument, "I'm sure if I call you, you can be back in under two minutes."

They locked gazes, neither speaking for several long seconds. He picked up his phone and texted Douglas, I'll meet you at the property line.

Sean prayed he wouldn't regret his decision to leave Jenna and help his only other neighbor.

THIRTEEN

Jenna twisted the dead bolt and then pressed her ear against the door. "Did you hear that?"

"Yes," Sean replied from the other side. "Leave it locked until I get home."

"Just go already. I'll be fine. Beau is here with me. You know he'll do a good job guarding me. And I have the rifle. I'm going to work on my podcast. Bye."

Once she heard the ATV motor start, she went to the guest bedroom and grabbed her laptop bag, her laptop, headphones and cell phone. Then she went back into the kitchen, where she placed everything on the table. Snagging a mug out of the cabinet, she poured a cup of coffee and settled in at the table, ready to work, with Beau at her feet. The house was exceptionally quiet, enabling her to hear every creak and moan as the wind howled outside.

"It's an old house, Jenna. Don't let your imagination run away with you." After opening a new tab on her computer, she navigated to her favorite music-streaming website and pulled up a playlist of soft instrumental jazz. Beau howled.

"Come on, boy. Surely you like good music." The coonhound laid his head on the floor and covered his face with a paw. She giggled. "Okay, I won't force you to listen to my music."

She pulled her laptop bag closer and dug around inside until her hand closed around her headphone case. Opening it, she pulled out one earbud and pressed it into her ear. She needed the noise to settle her nerves, but she still needed to listen for an intruder. Allowing the music to envelop her, she quickly got to work editing the bonus material she was adding to the end of the video clip.

Forty-five minutes later, she completed the last edit and initiated the video upload to the podcast host site. Standing, she rubbed the back of her neck, then crossed to the coffeepot and poured herself a fresh cup. Her phone rang, and she jumped with a start.

Picking the device up off the table, she looked at the screen. A local number scrolled across the top. She didn't recognize it. Probably a telemarketer. She ignored it and turned to her computer to check the upload progress. The ringing stopped, but then started again almost immediately. The same number. She slid her finger across the screen and answered the call. "Hello?"

"Ms. Hartley, it's Tristan. Tristan Kent. I hope... That is..."

He sounded out of breath, as if he'd been running. Her heart raced. What if he was in trouble because he had spoken to her yesterday? Could the killer be chasing him?

"Tristan, is something wrong? Where are you? Is someone trying to hurt you?"

"No, I'm okay. After I saw you yesterday, I started to think. And I need to talk to you, to tell you what I know."

"What do you mean?" She clutched the phone tighter. "Do you know who killed Becca?" If he knew something, why had he not told her before? She tamped down her anger and released a slow breath. "Tristan, if you know who killed Becca, tell me. They're after me now. My life is in danger."

"I know who's after you," he whispered. "I'll stop him before he can hurt you. I promise to protect you. For Becca." His voice cracked, and a sob came across the line.

"Don't do anything to put yourself in danger, Tristan. Just tell me who it is. I'll call Sheriff Dalton. He can arrest the person and put a stop to this, once and for all."

"No. I'll call the sheriff later. I promise. But I need to talk to you first. I need to explain why I didn't come forward sooner and tell you what I knew. But I need to do this in person. Is there any way you can meet me?"

"Of course. Just tell me where you are. I'm ready to put this nightmare behind me—well, I can't ever truly put it behind me, but I'm ready for answers. So Becca's death doesn't continue to consume me."

"I understand. And I'm ready to release the information I've been holding on to. I just hope you can forgive me for not telling you sooner. I should've told you yesterday, but I was afraid of what he would do if I did."

"Who is *he*?"

"I can't tell. Not yet."

"I won't let him hurt you, Tristan. Tell me where to meet you."

"You pick a spot. It needs to be somewhere he won't think to look for us. I don't want him finding us before I talk to the sheriff… We don't want to put others in danger, but I understand if you want to make it a public place. I know I'm asking a lot for you to meet me."

"Why don't we meet at the sheriff's office? We would be safe there. You could talk to me and Sheriff Dalton at the same time."

"No! Please. I need to explain everything to you first. I'll go straight to the sheriff, afterward, but *please* let me talk to you alone first."

"What if I bring Sean with me? He's the man you met yesterday. You can trust him."

"I won't talk with him. He's a former cop." The sound of someone knocking on a door came across the line, followed by the sound of a flushing toilet and running water. "I've gotta go," Tristan said in a hushed whisper.

"No, wait!" *Lord, I have to find out the truth about what happened to Becca. Please let Tristan be on the up and up, and don't let Sean be mad at me for leaving the house.* "I'll meet you. Meet me at Thatcher Park. There may be a few people at the playground, but in the back corner, there's a small parking area and a meditation memorial garden few people are aware of. I can be there in twenty minutes." This was the best compromise she could think of for a public meeting place that was still private.

"I know exactly where it is. I'll be there waiting for you."

Jenna disconnected the call and headed toward the door, then stopped. How was she going to get there? For a moment, she'd completely forgotten her truck had blown up. She didn't have a vehicle, and even if she could find a rental place that made deliveries in Barton Creek, there was no time.

Sean had driven his ATV to meet Douglas. His SUV was still here. She could *borrow* it. But where were the keys? *Think.* The first night she'd spent in his house, he'd hung his keys on a hook beside the pantry door. She quickly crossed the room. *Yes!* His keys dangled from a hook. She clutched them in her hand and raced for the front door with Beau at her heels, barking and nipping at her feet.

"Stop it, Beau."

The hound nipped at her again, caught her shoestring in his mouth and pulled, untying her shoes. She swatted him away with her hand and quickly retied her shoe. Then she looped her arm around the dog's neck and hugged him tight.

"It's going to be okay, boy. I promise. I know what I'm doing." He licked her cheek, and she buried her face in his furry neck. Did she really know what she was doing? Or was she being reckless? What advice would she give someone in her position?

She pushed to her feet and went back to the kitchen table. Grabbing the notepad and pen, she jotted down a note telling Sean exactly where she was going and who she was meeting. Then she grabbed a handful of dry dog food, carried it to the sunroom and dropped it into Beau's food bowl. He rushed over to it and ate, and she eased out of the room, closing the French door behind her. He looked up, whimpered and then turned back to his snack.

"I'm sorry, buddy, but I have to go."

Jenna turned and raced out the front door. She was finally going to get the answers she had been looking for.

Sweat ran down Sean's neck despite the temperature being a cool forty-seven degrees. He wiped it away with his gloved hand and squinted at the sun. They had been working for almost an hour and a half. He'd been gone much longer than he had expected. While Douglas had been correct and the fence was a quick repair, the job hadn't been small at all. A large fallen tree had needed to be cut away before they could repair the fence. Fortunately, the tree had missed the posts, so it would simply be a matter of pulling the barbed wire taut and reattaching it once they removed the last section of the tree. Hopefully, Sean would be headed home soon.

He turned to watch the chain saw in his neighbor's hands chew through a seven-inch-diameter limb. The bar broke through the wood, and the limb dropped to the ground. Douglas cut the motor on the chain saw, and Sean grabbed hold of the limb and pulled it off the barbed wire. Then both men stretched the barbed wire taut and fastened it into place.

Sean swung the hammer and drove his last fencing staple into place. He dropped the tool into the open toolbox and turned to Douglas. "I hate to leave you with all this cleanup, but I really need to get back to the house."

"I heard Jenna is staying at your place while the sheriff is trying to capture the person who has been attacking her."

Sean knew the older man wasn't trying to gossip or find out details from him concerning Jenna—it was more a matter of a neighbor showing concern. Still, he would never share the details of an open case with anyone. It wasn't ethical. Besides, even though he strongly suspected Douglas Anthony wasn't guilty of killing Becca, or trying to kill Jenna, he didn't know who was, so it was best to keep silent.

"Well, I'll get going."

"Tell Jenna the missus and I are praying for her." Douglas followed him to his ATV. "Keep her safe."

Sean nodded, straddled his ATV and raced across the field, the small vehicle bouncing over the terraces. He hoped Jenna had finished her podcast edits. He wanted to sit down with her and do some internet sleuthing. Maybe they could find Becca's classmates on social media and find connections between them and Becca, photos and whatnot, from around the time of her death. If so, the information could lead them to the killer.

He pulled the ATV up to the back of the house and parked it close to the patio. Turning off the motor, he dismounted and headed toward the back door. The minute he stepped onto the patio, Beau started howling. He sounded as if he were close by. Sean turned toward the sunroom and could see furry paws reaching up under the closed blinds, scratching at the windows.

The hairs on the back of Sean's neck stood at attention. Why was Beau in the sunroom? Had Jenna put him in there because he was bothering her while she worked? No. Surely not. If that had been the case, she would've let him free by now. His howling and scratching had to be more distracting to her work. Sean jogged to the back door and twisted the knob. Locked. He banged on the door. "Jenna! Jenna, let me in!"

Beau's cries grew louder, as if he were in great distress. Sean had to get inside. Was the spare key still where his grandmother had hidden it years ago? He stepped off the patio and crossed to the garden gnome that stood watch in his grandmother's flower bed. Picking up the figurine, he found the key embedded in the dirt beneath it. Snatching it up, he wiped it on his pants and ran back to the door.

He entered the kitchen. It was empty. Jenna's laptop sat on the table, a screen saver montage of photos flashing across the screen.

"Jenna, where are you? Answer me!" he yelled as he went from room to room.

No answer and no Jenna. Had the killer taken Jenna and locked Beau in the sunroom? It didn't feel or look like a crime scene. Knowing Jenna, if someone had abducted her, she wouldn't have gone without a fight. There would have been chairs knocked over or broken lamps or something. Instead, there was just a distraught Beau looking into the house from the other side of the French doors. Moving through the living room, Sean opened the door, and the coonhound darted out and made a beeline for the front door. Which was locked. A criminal wouldn't have taken the time to lock the house up before leaving. Jenna had left off her own free will. But she didn't have a vehicle. Unless...

He grasped the doorknob and fumbled with the lock. Finally, he unlocked the latch and yanked open the front door. Stepping outside, he looked at where he had parked his SUV last night. It was gone. She had taken his vehicle. But where was she? And why would she leave without telling him?

Sean stomped back into the house and made his way to the kitchen. He sat down at the table in front of her computer. Maybe he could find answers. He clicked a button, and the screen saver went away. But a password prompt replaced it. Now what?

Beau placed his front paws on his leg.

"Where did she go?" Sean asked, peering into the dog's sad eyes. "Too bad you can't answer me. Now, go. Let me think."

The coonhound slunk under the table, and Sean ducked to look at him lying on the floor. "I'm sorry, buddy. I know you're worried about her, too."

Straightening, Sean's shoulder connected with a notebook, knocking it to the floor. He bent to pick it up and was about to place it back on the table when the handwriting caught his attention. It was a note scribbled by Jenna.

> Sean, I'm sorry I had to leave without telling you. I've gone to meet Tristan. He knows who the killer is. Said he'd talk to Heath but wanted to talk to me first. Couldn't tell us anything yesterday because the killer was watching him. Meeting at Thatcher Park. Don't worry. I'll be back soon and fill you in. Jenna

He pushed his chair back and jumped to his feet. What was she thinking? How could she have gone without telling him? He knew the answer to that. She'd been afraid he wouldn't let her go alone. And he wouldn't have. Reaching into his back pocket, he pulled out his phone and dialed Heath.

As soon as the phone stopped ringing—before Heath had a chance to speak—Sean blurted, "Jenna's in trouble. You need to send help immediately."

"Is she at your house?"

"No, she went to Thatcher Park to meet Tristan Kent. He says he knows who killed Becca. I have a bad feeling."

"When did she leave? And why did you let her go alone?"

"I didn't. And I don't know when she left. I was helping Douglas with…" He puffed out a breath. "Look, I never dreamed that she would willingly leave to go meet someone. But she did. And she took my vehicle. So please send help."

"I can't. There was an accident involving a school bus on Rudd Hollow Road. My officers are out there directing traffic and dealing with the injured. And I'm on my way back from Sevierville."

Frustration bubbled up inside him. Sean had let down another woman who'd expected him to protect her. "Her life is in danger."

"Listen, Sean, Jenna is a smart woman. If she thought Tristan was a threat, she wouldn't have gone."

Sean didn't care that Jenna had felt safe. Felicia had felt safe, too, in her own driveway in a gated community. Sometimes, no matter the precautions one took, things still went terribly wrong. "How far are you from Barton Creek?"

"Ten minutes."

"Can you swing by and pick me up? I want to go with you."

"Sure. In the meantime, say a prayer for her safety."

Sean disconnected his phone and shoved it into his back pocket. *Lord, let Heath be right. Let Tristan be a good guy, and let Jenna be safe. Please. I beg of You.*

FOURTEEN

Jenna pulled Sean's SUV into the same parking space they had parked in two days ago—a green Jeep was two spaces away. There were no other vehicles in sight. Jenna exited the SUV, walked over to the Jeep and looked through the tinted windows. The vehicle was empty. There was a practice jersey in the passenger seat. This had to be Tristan's vehicle. Where was he? Had he gone for a walk in the memorial garden?

"Lord, don't let the person after me find us here. I don't know how I could ever live with the guilt if something happens to Tristan because he's helping me. Please guide my steps and protect us from the danger lurking in the shadows. If something happens to me, Sean will feel guilty, even though it won't be his fault. And, Lord, forgive me for trying to do this all on my own, and for not leaning on You for strength when I lost my sweet Becca. I now know that I can't get through any of life's bumps or heartaches without You."

Her phone rang, the sound piercing the silence. Sean's name flashed on the screen.

"Please don't answer it," Tristan said from behind her. Spinning around, she saw him standing beneath the arched entrance to the meditation garden. Jenna rejected the call with an automated text saying she couldn't talk right now. Then she pressed down on the small button on the side of the phone to silence it, not wanting to attract attention from others who were enjoying the playground area of the park.

"Okay. I've silenced my phone." She slipped it into her jacket pocket. "Do you want to talk in my vehicle?"

The young man shook his head. Then he turned and walked into the garden.

A calm peace she couldn't explain if she tried settled over her, and she trailed him.

They walked in silence until they reached a short wooden bridge that crossed a narrow creek. Tristan stopped and leaned against the railing, a sad expression on his face. "Becca loved this garden. Did you know she ate lunch here at least twice a month, no matter how warm or cold the weather was? She said that being in this garden brought her a sense of peace and that she thought it was the closest she'd ever get to the peace you felt when you would hike in the woods."

Tightness gripped Jenna's chest. How had she not known this about her own daughter? And why had Becca kept her friendship with Tristan a secret from her?

He locked gazes with her, and the pain she saw in the depths of his eyes chilled her to the core. "You were the person Becca had lunch with the day she died."

"Yes. It was our first and only date." Tears streamed down his face as loud sobs racked his body.

She tamped down the urge to comfort him and tell him it would be okay. Until she knew what happened to her daughter, her maternal instincts would have to remain dormant. "Did you kill Becca?"

"No! I could never have hurt her. I would have done anything to keep her safe. You'll never know how many times I've cried myself to sleep, begging God to turn back time and take me in her place."

If only it were possible to bring back the dead by offering to exchange places with them, Becca would've returned long ago because Jenna had made the same useless plea to God.

"Were you with her when she died?"

He opened his mouth, then closed it, and the muscle in his jaw twitched. Looking down at his hands, he whispered, "Forgive me, Lord." Then he turned toward Jenna, his gaze seemingly looking straight through her. And an icy shiver shook her entire body.

"It was my first year at college. The football practices and games were so time-consuming that I struggled to keep my grades up. It was Christmas break. I was only home for a few days because we had a bowl game. And I had to get back to campus for additional practices. But I was determined to get a head start on my assignments for the next semester. I was doing research and needed a book. So I came to the Maryville library to see if they had it, and Becca helped me. We'd had classes together in high school, but we never hung out with the same crowds. So I never really spoke to her until that day. She had the most beautiful smile I had ever seen. I flirted with her, and she brushed me off. But I was enamored with her, so every time I came home, I found an excuse to go to the library. I knew she would be there. We started talking and were amazed at the things we had in common.

Soon we became friends. We started chatting online, and I asked her out for Valentine's Day. But again, she turned me down. I was hurt, so I stayed away for a few weeks, and I ignored her when she reached out."

Nausea enveloped Jenna. How had she not known about any of this? Why hadn't Becca confided in her? She thought they had been close. That they'd had a relationship that most mothers and daughters could only dream of having. Had it all been a lie?

Her legs shook. "I need a place to sit down."

"There's a bench near the sand-and-rock garden." He reached for her arm. "Here, let me help you."

She dodged his grasp. "No! I can manage on my own."

He looked as if she had slapped him. She immediately regretted the pain she had caused him, but at that moment, her senses were on overload. And she could not bear the thought of him touching her.

They walked in silence. She had the sudden thought that going deeper into the garden with him was just leading her farther and farther away from help. Her steps faltered, and she stumbled on a patch of uneven ground. Tristan caught her, steadying her. She jumped back, his touch making her physically ill.

"I won't hurt you." He held up his hands, palms out, in surrender. "I understand why you don't want me to touch you, but I couldn't let you fall and get hurt. I wasn't able to keep one Hartley girl safe, and the pain and guilt have been more than I can endure. Once I finish telling you the story, I'll go straight to the sheriff. I will also avoid you at all costs in the future so you don't have to see me and I don't heap additional pain upon you."

More than he could endure? What about the pain she'd

gone through for nearly four years, not knowing what had happened to Becca? Had he never once thought about that—her never-ending pain? Tears burned her eyes, and her throat tightened. She moistened her lips. "Tell me what happened. I will listen and reserve judgment." She walked over to the bench, sat down and scooted to the opposite side, sitting on the edge.

He frowned and sat down, leaving two feet of space between them. "Becca called me and left me a voice message. She said that she really liked me and didn't want to lose my friendship. That she promised you she would get her college degree before she seriously dated. So she mostly just hung out with people in groups, and she was afraid if she allowed herself to go on a date with me, she might not be able to keep her promise to you. If she stopped thinking we were just friends, she was sure she would fall in love...with me."

He picked at the side seam of his blue jeans. "I told her I understood because I was already falling for her."

A cloud drifted in front of the sun, and the shadows deepened in the grove of bamboo to their left.

"We agreed to keep in touch via text and to not see each other in person because the temptation to want to go on a date and see where the relationship would go would be too great."

"Why didn't I see any text messages between you when I looked through Becca's phone?" she blurted out, unable to stop herself.

"My middle name is Jordan. I asked Becca to use that name in her phone for me because I knew if you saw it, you would think the person sending the text was a girl.

But we also always texted through an app that deletes the messages as soon as they have been read. I'm sorry."

He grimaced. "My aunt Harriet used to say nothing good will ever come from a lie or a deception. Oh, how I wish I would have heeded her words. If I had, maybe Becca would be alive today."

A twig snapped, and a red fox scurried out of the trees and across the bridge. Jenna placed her hand on her chest, willing her heartbeat to slow. She released a long breath. "What happened that day? Why did y'all decide to meet that afternoon if y'all had previously decided to not see each other in person again?"

"I had—"

"Stop right there, Tristan." Coach David Kent stepped out of the woods, a pistol in his hands. "I told you I'd handle this. Now, you need to get out of here. Go home. Let me take care of things."

"No, sir." Tristan scooted closer to Jenna and placed a hand on her arm, his eyes never leaving his father. "I told you, it's past time for me to own up to my mistakes. It's long overdue."

"But you did nothing wrong. *You* didn't kill Becca," David insisted. "She wouldn't have wanted you to give up your education or your chance at the pros because of her clumsiness."

He was blaming Becca for her own death? An involuntary gasp escaped Jenna, drawing David's ire. He took a step forward, raising his weapon and peering through the sights.

Tristan jumped between Jenna and his dad, positioning himself so that he shielded her with his body. "I didn't report what happened all those years ago because of *you*.

It was wrong. I constantly wonder, if I'd called the sheriff instead of listening to you that afternoon, how different my life would be."

"You're right—your life *would* be different. For starters, you would have lost your scholarship to college. Do you think the university would have held the spot open, waiting for you while you went on trial to defend yourself? Of course they wouldn't have. Which also means you would not be slated to be picked in the NFL—"

"I *will not* be part of the draft, Dad. I'm going to do what I should have done four years ago." Holding his hand out as if he were approaching a wounded animal, Tristan took two steps toward his father. "It's time for me to go to the sheriff's office and come clean about what happened the day Becca died."

"No!" David bellowed. "I've worked too hard to get you to this point. I won't let you throw it away over a reckless schoolgirl and her nosy mother. Now, go home and let me clean up your mess, again."

"Like you *cleaned it up* last time? I don't think so," Tristan said through clenched teeth.

Jenna scooted half-off, half-on the bench and looked around for anything that might be used as a weapon. A large rock the size of a softball lay on the ground just out of her reach. Moving slowly so she wouldn't draw attention to herself, she slipped off the bench and inched toward the rock.

"You'll have to shoot me to shoot her," Tristan said firmly. Hurrying footsteps sounded behind her.

She wrapped her hand around the rock and turned. Tristan shifted, once again blocking her from his dad.

Jenna stood, the rock firmly in her hands, not sure how it would be a match for a gun, but it was all she had.

"Move, Tristan. It's time for this to end. Once and for all," David bellowed.

"You're right, it is. But it won't end this way, Dad." The football player she'd enjoyed watching run plays through the years turned and snatched the rock from her hands. Then he whirled around and threw it, knocking the gun out of his dad's hand. The weapon flew into a juniper bush.

Coach Kent dove after his weapon, and Tristan grabbed Jenna's hand, and they ran in the opposite direction, deeper into the meditation garden.

Dear Lord, there's nowhere to hide. Had Sean found her note? Was help on the way?

FIFTEEN

"Can't you go any faster?" Sean probed. "I still don't understand why you aren't using your lights and siren."

Heath accelerated as the broken yellow line of a passing zone came into view. "I already told you. I won't run sirens on a curvy two-lane country road unless I know it is an emergency." He glided into the left lane, overtook the older gentleman in the sedan they had been following for the last five miles and maneuvered back into the right lane, well ahead of meeting the oncoming vehicle.

"How is this not an emergency?" Sean bit out through gritted teeth.

"Look, Sean, I realize you've formed a close attachment to Jenna the past few days, but don't tell me how to do my job. She *chose* to leave your home, *borrow* your SUV and *meet* Tristan. The people driving on this road today didn't ask her to do any of those things. The road is curvy, with minimal straight sections, and there are no pull-offs. If I activate my siren, the other drivers are likely to speed up— thinking they are helping me get to my destination more quickly—take a curve too fast and crash. Which means it would take us even longer to get to Jenna, and an innocent person could lose their life."

Sean drummed his fingers on his leg. Heath was right

to not take unnecessary risks that put innocent people in danger, but the thought of Jenna being out there alone with a killer... No. He couldn't let his mind go there. Jenna would be okay. She was a smart woman, and she had done a good job of taking care of herself all these years.

It suddenly hit him that he didn't want her to always have to be strong and independent. He wanted to be the one to take care of her. To nurture her. To protect her. To help her solve all the cold case crimes she desired. To love her.

He didn't know how she would feel about his newly discovered feelings, if she would open her heart to the possibility that they could be more than neighbors. If they could see where their budding friendship could lead them. After all, according to Grandma Lois, great love stories always start with friendship. Could Jenna possibly have similar feelings for him? Bouncing his leg, he itched to get out of the slow-moving vehicle and run. Because at the moment, the adrenaline coursing through his body made him feel as if he could fly.

Sean's phone rang, and Jenna's name flashed across the screen. "Thank You, Lord."

He pressed the button to answer and immediately placed the call on speaker. "Jenna, are you okay?"

"No... Sean, help," she whispered, urgency punctuating her words. "He has a gun. He's going to kill me."

"Tristan?"

"No, Coach... I mean David. David Kent." Unintelligible, whispered words sounded in the background. "Tristan, no. Stay with me. Don't go out there. Tristan!"

Accelerating, Heath activated the emergency lights and siren.

Sean gripped the phone tighter. "Jenna we're almost there." Turning to Heath, he added, "How long?"

"Less than five minutes." Heath palmed his radio and called Dispatch for backup.

"Did you hear that? We're almost there."

"Please hurry." The fear in her voice reached out and squeezed his lungs like a vise.

He inhaled deeply and slowly exhaled. "Can you tell me what's happening?"

"Tristan is trying to lead his father away from me. I'm hiding in the gazebo. Sean, please hurry." Her voice cracked, and a sob sounded across the line.

Heath weaved in and out of traffic. "Jenna, stay hidden and stay on the line. And stay perfectly still and quiet."

"Is your phone pressed to your ear?" Sean asked.

"Earbud," she whispered softly.

He smiled. "Smart thinking. I can keep talking to you, and you won't feel so alone. Make sure you have all sounds muted on your phone, though. You don't want a text message or something giving away your location."

Silence settled over the line. He missed the connection to her voice, letting him know she was still okay. But as long as she was silent, there was less risk of the killer finding her.

The entrance to the park came into view. "We're almost there, Jenna."

Heath turned into the parking lot, lights and sirens blaring, and zoomed past the main playground area. Parents grabbed their children and pulled them close, staring at the scene. A deputy's vehicle pulled in behind them. Heath spoke into his radio and ordered the deputy to instruct the families to evacuate the property and then to block the entrance to the back parking lot, not allowing spectators into what was likely to be a very dangerous situation.

Sean wished he had been smart enough to bring his own headphones, but he hadn't. He didn't want to disconnect the call, but he would have to at this point. "Jenna, I have to hang up. I will get to you as quickly as I can."

"I understand." The line went dead. It felt as if someone had reached into his chest and pulled out his heart.

Heath parked, and Sean went to open his door. Heath placed a hand on his arm. "Do you have a weapon?"

"Of course I do." Sean palmed his Glock and exited the vehicle, then rounded the front and met Heath on the path that led to Jenna.

"You know I shouldn't let a civilian be involved in this. If things go haywire, I could be in a lot of trouble."

"Try to stop me."

"That's what I figured. We're going to separate. Head toward the gazebo and get Jenna. I'm going to circle the other way and see if I can find Tristan and his dad. If you see anything, yell. I'll come running. But be aware, as my other deputies arrive, they'll be in these woods as well."

"You forget I'm not a rookie. I've been doing this longer than you have. Now, it's time to find this guy and end this today." They crossed under the entrance archway, and Sean went left while Heath went right.

Sean had never explored the meditation garden. He was reliant upon the signs to point him in the direction he needed to go. His feet crunched on the gravel as he ran, and he moved off the path to the grassy area, racing toward the unknown. *Lord, don't let me be too late.*

Sounds from the parking area reached Jenna's hiding spot, Sirens clashed with the screams of children, and she could only imagine the chaos. Her heart raced, and sweat beaded her hairline. Wrapping her arms around her body, she huddled against the gazebo wall. *Help is on the way. Sean is almost here.* Over and over, she repeated the silent mantra in her head. *Sean will save me. He won't let David get to me first.*

"Dad, it's over." Tristan yelled from somewhere to her right. "Dad, come out wherever you're hiding. Come out and turn yourself in," Tristan pleaded. "I'm sorry. I know I let you down. I wish I could go back four years and undo everything. But I can't. What I can do is stop you from making things worse."

A twig snapped behind her, and she gasped. Clamping her hand over her mouth, she prayed that if the noise had been David, he hadn't heard her. *Hurry, Sean.*

A firm hand grabbed her by the hair and jerked her upward. She cried out and twisted, looking into the eyes of her tormentor.

David threw a leg over the low wall of the gazebo and climbed over to stand next to her, his grip on her hair never wavering. She flailed around, swinging her arms and trying to break free. He pressed his gun to her side, let go of her hair and slid his left arm around her neck. She clawed at his hands. He tightened his grasp, cutting off her airway. Dizziness descended upon her, and a whooshing sound clogged her ears. She was going to pass out. *No.* Jenna couldn't allow the darkness to win.

If someone grabs you from behind, instantly go into the turtle position—neck down, shoulders up. If that fails, execute a drop and flip. A long-forgotten self-defense video clip she'd shared with her viewers in one of her early podcasts suddenly came to mind. Too late for the turtle position. She'd have to try the other maneuver. *Lord, don't let the gun go off.*

Tilting sideways, she dropped to her left knee. David lost his grasp on her throat, and the gun clattered to the floor. Scrambling to the wall, she clawed her way upward as she inhaled large gulps of air, desperate to relieve her burning lungs.

"No!" David grasped her hair, jerked her around and backhanded her across the face. "You will not get away that easily. You and your daughter have ruined my son's life. All my son's dreams have been taken away. All because of a clumsy girl and her ridiculous podcast mom."

Tears stung Jenna's eyes. *Ignore the pain. Focus on escaping.* Blindly, she kicked and swatted at him. He let go of her hair. She landed on her backside. David bent over her and reached for her legs. She drew back and kicked as hard as she could, connecting with the one area that was sure to bring him to his knees. He convulsed in pain and fell against the railing. She scooted backward, never taking her eyes off him. Splinters dug into her palms, and she bit the inside of her cheek. *Don't stop. Keep moving.*

Jenna pulled her knees close, flipped over, her feet flat on the floor, and pushed upward, then leaped off the gazebo, clearing both steps. She raced toward one of the two bridges that connected the small island the gazebo was on with the land encircling the pond.

A gunshot rang out. She startled, missing a step. The toe of her left foot connected with the wooden deck floor of the bridge, and she plunged toward the cold water below.

"Heath, over here!" Sean raced along the trail that wound through the trees in the direction the gunshot had sounded from. He burst into the clearing just in time to see Jenna crawl out of the pond and collapse onto the small island. David Kent stood inches away with a gun pointed at her. Why hadn't she swam to the other side?

Sean raised his Glock. "Drop your weapon, Kent. It's over," he commanded, inching closer to the bridge with small half steps, his eyes never leaving the football coach. He desperately wanted to rush to Jenna. If she wasn't able to get out of the wet clothing quickly and warm up, she would be at risk of hypothermia.

In one swift move, David pulled Jenna to her feet and positioned her in front of him as a shield. "Don't come any closer, Quinn."

Movement on the other side of the pond caught his attention. Heath had made his way to the other bridge. Sean's heart jumped into his throat. One wrong move and David would kill Jenna. *Keep him talking.*

"You don't really want to do this. You're throwing away your career. Do you really want to spend life in prison—or worse, receive the death penalty?"

"Dad!"

Tristan darted past Sean and raced onto the small island. "It's over. Please do as Mr. Quinn asked." The young man cast a quick glance over his shoulder. "Stay behind me."

"Can't do that," Sean replied through clenched teeth. He would not allow someone else to shield him. "I won't have my view *or* my shot blocked."

"Please give me a chance to resolve this," Tristan whispered. He turned back to his father. "Ms. Hartley did nothing wrong, Dad. She simply wanted answers, like any parent would. When I heard about the attacks on her,

I knew you were behind them. And I knew I had to stop you."

"You should've stayed at college. You have several busy months ahead of you, with the NFL draft and then finals."

"I've withdrawn from the draft."

Pain etched the coach's face. "No!" he bellowed. "Why?"

Tears streamed down Tristan's cheeks. "Because it was the only way I could stop you and put an end to this. And because it was time—actually, *past* time—to give Ms. Hartley answers. Keeping quiet about what happened that day hasn't been fair to anyone. Not to Becca's memory. Not to me. And not to you."

David tightened his hold on Jenna. Her eyes widened. "You're wrong. What isn't fair is you throwing away everything we've worked for. Why are you throwing your dreams away?"

Heath rounded the gazebo, his weapon fixed on David.

Tristan took a step closer to his father. "Besides teaching me how to be the best football player, you also taught me to be an honorable man. Somewhere along the way, you decided fame and glory were more important than honor. But I don't believe that. I will not dishonor Becca's memory any longer by staying quiet."

Two sheriff's deputies stepped into the clearing with guns drawn.

"Drop your weapon, Coach Kent. You're surrounded," Heath instructed, making his presence known.

The coach turned his head from side to side, taking in the scene that had unfolded, realization dawning on his face. He let go of Jenna, and she collapsed to the ground at his feet.

Tristan went to his father and gently pried the gun from

his hands, then handed it to Heath. "We'll turn ourselves in together. Okay, Dad?"

Sean raced across the bridge and gathered Jenna into his arms as Heath and the deputies handcuffed the two men. She shivered. Sean shrugged out of his coat and wrapped it around her shoulders.

"Do…do they have to cuff Tristan? He saved my life," Jenna asked, burying her face in Sean's neck.

"It's okay," Tristan assured her.

Heath jerked his head, signaling to the deputies. "Okay, guys, let's get these two to the station." He met Sean's gaze. "After she's had a chance to change and warm up, I need you to bring her in so she can give a statement."

Sean nodded, then turned his attention back to the woman in his arms. "Do you think you can walk?"

"Yes." She looked up, remorse written in her eyes. "I'm sorry I—"

Her bottom lip quivered. And, as if he were being pulled by an unseen magnetic field, he lowered his head and captured her mouth with his. She wrapped her arms around his waist, the kiss deepening ever so slightly.

When he was completely out of breath, he pulled back and stood. "If we don't get moving, you're going to catch hypothermia."

"Not if you keep kissing me like that," she said.

They had a lot to discuss before they got lost in each other's kisses. But later. For now, Sean had to be the voice of reason. "I'm afraid kisses won't be enough to keep you from catching a cold—or worse, pneumonia. So humor me, and let me get you to my warm vehicle quickly."

Sean kissed the top of her damp head. He placed an arm around her shoulders and slid the other under her knees. Then he scooped her up into his arms and made his way across the bridge. Closing her eyes, she rested her head against his chest. Their hearts beat in rhythm. After the trauma she'd endured, he couldn't be sure what the exchange meant to her. Did she share his feelings? Or was she simply accepting his embrace because she needed comfort? He'd have to be patient a little longer to find out. There were more important things to deal with first.

SIXTEEN

Heath met them as they entered the station. "Are you okay? Do you need to see a doctor?" he asked Jenna, concern in his eyes.

She shook her head. "No. I'll be fine."

"Are they opening up about Becca's death, or have they lawyered up?" Sean asked, obviously ready to get down to business.

"David Kent has called his lawyer. We're waiting for him to arrive so we can continue our questioning. Tristan, on the other hand, wants to tell his story. But he has requested Jenna be in the room."

"No. Absolutely not." Sean shoved his hand through his hair.

"That's my call, don't you think?" She met his gaze and refused to look away.

He puffed out of breath. "Yes, of course. But don't you think you've been through enough? That kid allowed you to live in torment for nearly four years. Do you really want—"

"What I want," she said softly, "is to know what happened to my precious Becca and why she had to die alone in the woods."

"Okay, then, although this is very unorthodox, I will

allow you to be in the room during his questioning. Tristan requested a court-appointed attorney. So he will be present during the interrogation." Heath put a hand on her upper back and turned her toward a long hallway. "If you'll come this way."

"I'm coming, too. I believe I've earned the right, being part of this investigation and all." Sean fell into step beside Jenna.

"Not so fast. I know you want to be there, but I can't risk the kid clamming up if you are." Heath paused beside a closed door. "So this is as far as I will allow you to go."

"But—"

"You'll see and hear everything on the monitors. But Tristan won't be able to see you," Heath insisted.

"Sean, I appreciate all you've done and how you've protected me and kept me alive these past four days. I know you want to be there for me for moral support, and I appreciate that." Becca raised her hand, catching herself before she caressed his face, and placed it on his arm. "This is something I have to do without you." She turned to Heath. "I'm ready."

They left Sean standing there. Heath led her a little farther down the hall and into an interrogation room.

Tristan sat at a small oblong table beside a man wearing a button-up shirt and tie with a bored expression on his face. When Tristan saw Jenna, he brightened. "Ms. Hartley, you're here. My dad didn't hurt you, did he?"

"No, I'm fine. How are you?" It felt odd to exchange pleasantries in this small interrogation room with the person who had been with Becca the day she died. But she needed him to feel at ease so he would open up about that day.

"I'm sorry I didn't tell you what I knew sooner. It's my fault that my dad tried to kill you."

The bored-looking gentleman sat up straight. "I told you not to volunteer any information."

"And I told you I'm not keeping secrets any longer. I'll face whatever consequences come my way."

Heath looked to the other gentleman. "May I proceed?"

The man shrugged. "Sure, but I want it noted that my client is answering your questions against my counsel."

"So noted." There was a knock on the door. Heath opened it and accepted two folding chairs from a deputy. "Thanks." He placed the chairs next to each other on the opposite side of the table from Tristan and his lawyer.

The deputy backed out of the cramped space, closing the door behind him. Jenna took in her surroundings, observing a camera near the ceiling in the corner. Was Sean watching, or had he left? No, he wouldn't leave. He'd proven the past four days that he was a loyal neighbor and friend. Heat warmed her cheeks as she remembered the kiss they had shared earlier. She must have seemed like a helpless, lost soul in that moment for him to feel the need to offer her such comfort. And she had most likely cemented that impression when she'd allowed him to carry her in his arms, snuggling in like a child hungry for affection.

"Jenna." Heath touched her shoulder and brought her back to the moment at hand. "Are you sure you're up to this?"

"Yes." She settled into the chair closest to the door and folded her hands in her lap. Nothing would get her out of this room until she finally knew why her precious daughter had been killed.

* * *

Sean leaned close and examined the image of the interrogation room displayed on the thirty-inch monitor. Jenna looked as if she might pass out. He knew this was too much for her. He should've insisted on Heath postponing the interrogation until tomorrow, giving Jenna a little time to recover from the ordeal of the morning. Of course, he had no rights to demand anything. And if the cold shoulder Jenna had given him since the shared kiss was any indication, he never would have rights to voice his opinion about what she should or shouldn't do for her own well-being ever again.

He was angry with himself for not reading the situation correctly. Sean should've realized that she was in shock following the near-death experience and falling into the cold pond.

He had always heard hindsight was twenty-twenty. In this case, it definitely was. But he couldn't go back and change things. All he could do was pray that she would allow him to explain and to declare his intentions. He chuckled. Sean could hear his grandpa now. "It's important to not let your wishes and desires lead you around. Always make sure your intentions are honorable."

The door opened, and Deputy Moore stepped into the room. "You look pretty happy for someone watching an interrogation."

Sean shook his head. "No. Just remembering something my grandpa always said to me."

The deputy raised an eyebrow but did not comment.

"Are you here to watch with me?"

"Yes. It's standard procedure. I'm sure you understand."

Sean turned his attention back to the monitor.

"As I was telling Ms. Hartley before my dad showed up…" Tristan slammed his fist on the table and Jenna jumped. "I don't know how I could've been so reckless. I should've known Dad would follow me today, just like he did that day."

"I will not tolerate an outburst like that, young man. Do you understand?" Heath growled angrily.

"Yeah, I'm sorry." The young man turned to Jenna. "Sorry."

"Continue." Heath motioned for Tristan to carry on.

"The day Becca died. We were on our first date. We went on a picnic and had a nice time. Originally, that was all we were going to do, but Becca said her mom was visiting her aunt and wouldn't be home for several hours, so we went hiking. We left Becca's car at the meditation garden. I drove us to my house, where I picked up a daypack, a couple of protein bars and a couple of waters, and then we went to the hiking trail."

"Was anyone at home when you went by there?" Heath inquired.

Tristan shook his head. "No. My dad had taken my mother for a chemo treatment."

Jenna reached across the table and placed a hand on Tristan's. "I heard your mom passed away last year. I'm sorry."

Her ability to be so forgiving and offer sympathy to the person who was most likely responsible for Becca's death amazed Sean.

"Thank you," Tristan replied.

"Back to your story," Heath redirected the young man. "Please continue."

"We reached the hiking trail and hiked the ridge for

better views. When we reached the overlook, I wanted to climb out to Eagle Point and see what the views were like from there."

"Didn't you see the warning signs?" Heath leaned closer.

"Yes, sir. But I thought nothing would happen." Tristan shook his head. "How many people have had that very thought right before tragedy?"

Silence descended upon the interrogation room, and after several long seconds, Tristan continued. "Becca didn't want to go out to the end of Eagle Point, and I teased her for being a goody-goody. I told her…" His voice cracked, and tears ran down his face. "I told her I wouldn't let anything happen to her." He lowered his head, and his shoulders shook as he openly sobbed.

Jenna whispered something to Heath, and he pulled out his phone and typed a message.

Deputy Moore's cell phone buzzed. He read the text message and turned for the door.

"What's going on?" Sean asked.

"Ms. Hartley has requested water. I'll be right back."

The deputy left the room, and Sean turned back to stare at the woman who had stolen his heart.

There was a knock on the door. Heath got up to answer it, and Jenna followed him. "Can we talk outside just for a moment?"

He looked at her quizzically and nodded. Then he opened the door, accepted the bottle of water and passed it to Tristan. "We'll be right back."

They stepped into the hall to find Sean already waiting on them. "What's going on?"

"Jenna asked to speak with me." Heath gave him a pointed look. "In private."

Sean bristled.

"It's fine. You can stay," Jenna said, then turned to Heath. "I know that you've already bent the rules for me—and I hate to ask this—but could you and the lawyer maybe go into the viewing room and let me talk to Tristan alone?"

"You can't do that!" Sean's tone made it clear he didn't approve.

She spun around to face him. "If you want to stay in the observation room and listen, that's fine, but you don't get to have input here."

He looked as if someone had punched him in the gut, and she instantly regretted her words. She knew he meant well, but there was no way he could understand what she had been through the last four years and how desperate she was to have the answers she had been searching for. How much longer could she sit and watch as Tristan cried? She needed to put the young man at ease so he could get the story out quickly. Dragging it out was excruciating.

"I'll allow it." Heath laughed. "If for no other reason, then the fact that I've never seen anyone make my good buddy speechless."

Sean grunted, turned and went back into the viewing room. Jenna would have to mend fences with her neighbor later, or they would go back to the cold, not-so-neighborly relationship they had shared for the past six months.

"Thanks, Heath."

The sheriff searched her eyes. "Are you sure about this?"

She nodded.

"Okay, but I cannot force his lawyer to leave the room. If he refuses, I'm not leaving, either. Got it?"

"Sounds fair."

They reentered the room. Tristan had drunk some of the water and seemed to have regained his composure.

The lawyer sat with his legs straight out, crossed at the ankles, and his arms folded over his chest with his chin tucked in and his eyes closed. Had the man fallen asleep?

Heath gently kicked the sole of the lawyer's shoe, and he opened one eye. "Ms. Hartley has requested to speak to Tristan alone. And I am inclined to allow it."

The lawyer sat up straighter. "I object."

"I don't believe anyone is asking your permission," replied Tristan. Then he jerked his head toward the camera in the corner, near the ceiling on the far wall. "If I'm not mistaken, this room and all that is going on inside is being video recorded."

"That's correct," Heath affirmed.

"Who will watch our conversation?"

"Currently, there is a deputy and Sean Quinn watching the monitor. If you agree to talk to Ms. Hartley alone, your lawyer and I will watch the monitor along with Mr. Quinn, and I will station the deputy outside this door."

"I have no objection to that," Tristan stated.

His lawyer got up and stormed out of the room. Heath hugged Jenna. "If you need me, just give a signal, and I'll be back in here immediately," he whispered. Then he pulled back and followed the lawyer.

Jenna sat across from Tristan at the small table. "I know this is very emotional for you. You've had to keep everything bottled up for so long. You told me you didn't kill Becca, and I believe you." She inhaled deeply and then pushed out the breath slowly. "Did your dad kill my daughter?"

"No. Yes. Ugh." He pressed the heels of his palms against his temples. "His actions caused the accident, but he didn't plan to kill her."

"Why don't you tell me what you know? Then the sheriff can sort everything out." The urge to grasp him by the shoulders and shake the story out of him welled up inside her. She bit the corner of her lip and waited.

"I told you we went out to the rocks known as Eagle Point. We took our time and moved slowly so that we wouldn't fall. And after we made it to the tree, we sat down on the ground with our feet dangling over the edge. We were probably there for about thirty minutes, talking and finding out about each other."

"What did y'all talk about?" Jenna knew that Tristan and Becca's conversation had nothing to do with the case, but she needed to know. It was that simple.

Tristan frowned. "Nothing of significance. Normal things that people discuss when they're trying to get to know each other. Favorite color. Favorite music. Hobbies. School. We discussed my upcoming awards banquet. I asked if she would think about allowing me to talk to you and ask for permission to invite her to attend as my date."

"Her response?"

"She said she would think about it, but that even if she decided it would be okay, not to get my hopes up because you would never allow her to go on a solo date." He fidgeted with his fingernails.

Jenna squirmed in her seat. Sean, Heath and the attorney had just heard how she had failed as a mom, placing her own insecurities and past mistakes on her daughter.

Lord, I'm glad You are forgiving and are able to over-look my shortcomings. Because I'm afraid it will take me a long time to forgive myself.

"I'm sorry, I shouldn't have told you that," Tristan said softly. "You were a wonderful mom, everyone knows that. Becca never once spoke negatively about you. She loved you, and she wanted you to be proud of her. I know you were... *Are.*"

"Let's get back to what happened to Becca. You said y'all made it out there safely and sat near the tree. Then what?"

"My dad found us. I was supposed to be at the gym with some of my teammates who were also home for the weekend. Dad had taken Mom for her chemo treatment, so I figured what he didn't know wouldn't hurt him. Or me." Tristan pushed to his feet and paced. "I knew he had a tracking app on my phone. It's been on there since I was old enough to drive. He said it was for my protection. If anything happened to me, he would know where to look. But I knew it was so he could keep tabs on me. I was naive to think that he wouldn't check the app since he was busy with Mom, but he did. After he took Mom home from her treatment, he tracked me to the hiking trail. The sun was going down, so we had just headed back and were making our way across the uneven ground when Dad showed up on the other side of the fence and yelled at me. His sudden appearance and tone of voice startled Becca, and she stepped back. Only, when she did, she went over the edge. I tried to grab her, but it all happened so fast."

Tears sprang to Jenna's eyes, and she sucked in her breath. Oh, her sweet Becca. She wiped her eyes, desperate to stop the flow.

The door to the interrogation room flew open, and Heath and Sean burst into the room.

"I'll take over from here," Heath said. He glanced over his shoulder at Sean. "Get her out of here."

Sean gave a curt nod and started toward her.

"One moment… Please. I need to know one more thing." She held up a hand, halting Sean in his steps, and turned back to Tristan. "Why didn't you call for an ambulance?"

"At first, we didn't have cell service. We raced to the spot where she landed. Dad pushed me aside to check her pulse and said it was weak. Then he said he'd be right back and took off toward the parking area. Ten minutes later, he came back and said he had called 911 and ordered me to go home. He said Mom had already been left alone too long after a treatment. I told him I wasn't leaving until I knew Becca was okay. But he promised he'd take care of her and reminded me he was the only one of us certified in CPR. I left… But I only made it a couple hundred yards and turned around. I couldn't leave Becca …" Tristan sank onto the chair he'd vacated earlier. "As I came closer, I saw Dad…twist Becca's neck."

Jenna gasped, and Sean put a hand on her shoulder.

The court appointed lawyer tried to hush Tristan, but he continued as if in a trance watching a replay of the events. "I confronted him, and he said her injuries had been fatal. That she was suffering, and the ambulance wouldn't get there in time. I was in shock, so when he told me, once more, to go home and take care of Mom, I did. It wasn't until late the next day that I found out he hadn't actually reported it and Becca's body had been found by a couple of thru-hikers. When I asked him why he hadn't called it in, he said it was to protect me from a scandal that would cost me my football scholarship and a career in pro football. And to protect my mom from undue stress during an already-stressful time with cancer treatments. He said what happened had been an accident and sacrificing my *life* wouldn't bring Becca back."

Jenna stood, her entire body shaking, and turned to Sean. "I'm ready to go." He held out his hand. She placed her hand into his and focused on putting one foot in front of the other.

"I'm sorry, Ms. Hartley," Tristan whispered. "I'm sorry that I talked Becca into the hike that day. I'm sorry that my dad tracked us there. Most of all, I'm sorry we couldn't do anything to save her."

Grasping the doorframe with her free hand, she turned back to the tormented young man. "That's where you're wrong. She would have survived if only you or your dad had called 911."

"What do you mean?"

"After I received the autopsy report, I reached out to Dr. Langston—a doctor of internal medicine at Vanderbilt. She looked over the report of injuries. And she said *if* Becca's neck had not been broken and she had made it to the hospital within an hour of the accident, she would have had a ninety percent chance of survival. Every hour after that, that treatment was delayed, her chances would have diminished by fifty percent. Until she succumbed to her injuries." Jenna locked eyes with Tristan. "There's a good chance Becca would have been paralyzed from the waist down, but she didn't have to die."

Tristan recoiled as if he'd touched a live wire. "The

doctor has to be wrong. Dad said Becca's injuries were fatal. That's why he sent me away."

"He sent you away so he could murder my child and protect you from any fallout from the accident. Nothing— not even a young girl's life—mattered more to your dad than you becoming a pro football player." Jenna frowned and shook her head. Then she glanced at Heath. "Dr. Langston said she'd be willing to testify in court."

Tristan's face blanched. He ran to the trash can and became violently ill.

Sean put his hand on the small of Jenna's back and guided her out of the room. They made their way to Sean's vehicle in silence.

"Would you mind dropping me off at the rental-car place on Wisteria Street?" Jenna asked as Sean pulled out of the parking lot.

He looked as if he might argue, but then he nodded. "Okay."

"Thank you." She looked out the side window. "I thought I'd get a hotel room tonight and then look for a rental to-morrow."

"There's no need for that." He activated his blinker and slowed to turn into the car-rental parking lot. "You can stay at my house until you find a place."

"But I don't need to be protected now, and it wouldn't look right for us to share your home."

"I'll move into the camper until you find a rental." He pulled into a parking space.

"I don't know. It's been a stressful day. I really need time alone to decompress."

"You shall have it. I'll move into the camper before you

get back to the house. You won't see me the rest of the evening," Sean promised. "I'll even keep Beau with me."

How could she say no? He would think she was ungrateful for all he'd done. "Okay. Thank you." She smiled. "Beau can stay in the house with me."

Sean's deep, rich laughter followed her as she exited the vehicle, and her heart skipped a beat. She had gotten too comfortable being around him. But she *would* find a new place to live tomorrow. Put distance between her and her handsome neighbor so they could go back to being... what? Acquaintances? Friends? Jenna wasn't sure what their future relationship would look like, but she knew better than to hold out dreams of something more based on one kiss after a near-death experience.

SEVENTEEN

Sean stretched and massaged his lower back with his fingertips. He really needed to invest in a more comfortable mattress for the bed in his camper, especially since he hoped to convince Jenna to stay in his home until hers was repaired. Although he knew the probability was slim, he hoped she'd hear him out and consider the idea. He wanted to be there for her, to be a shoulder for her to lean on and to ensure she knew, even though they had captured the ones responsible for Becca's death, she wasn't in this alone. If she would allow it, he would be there with her through the court trials and all that would come after that.

What time is it? Trying to be mindful of Jenna's request for space to decompress, he would prefer not to go into the house unless he knew she was awake. He swung his feet to the floor and reached for his cell phone on the small built-in side table. 11:15 a.m. It was almost noon!

Jumping to his feet, Sean scrubbed a hand over his face and went to his tiny closet. He could not remember the last time he'd slept this late—probably not since his college days. He'd had difficulty shutting off his thoughts the night before and hadn't drifted off to sleep until after three, but he'd thought he'd only slept a couple of hours. Grabbing the jeans and long-sleeved pullover he'd hung up the night before, he quickly dressed. Surely Jenna was awake by now.

He shoved his feet into his boots, grabbed his denim jacket off the dinette table and headed out the door. The sun was shining brightly, the temperature warmer than it had been in months. It was going to be a beautiful day.

Whistling a tune, he made his way to the back door. He twisted the knob. Locked. Was Jenna still asleep? Maybe she'd had difficulty going to sleep, too. Sean had promised himself he wouldn't go into the house until he knew she was awake, because he didn't want Jenna to feel like he was hovering. Of course, Beau was probably pacing the floor, ready to go outside and relieve himself. He'd just go inside and take care of Beau, and then he'd slip back outside and enjoy the sunshine until she woke.

He shoved his hand into his pocket and retrieved his keys. Once inside, silence greeted him. Beau rested on the floor under the table. The coonhound lifted his head, looked at Sean with sad eyes, bawled and then lowered his head again.

"What's wrong, boy?" Sean crossed the room, his steps faltering when he spotted an envelope addressed to him on the table. Dropping his keys onto the table, he snatched the envelope and tore into it.

Sean,
Words will never be enough to express my gratitude for all you have done for me these last few days. You provided a safe haven in the midst of a storm for me, and I will forever be grateful. I'm sorry I didn't get to say goodbye in person, but I didn't want to disturb you. I'll be in touch.

Many thanks,
Jenna
P.S. I fed Beau and let him outside to play for thirty
minutes this morning.

He crumpled the paper in his fist, pressed it into a ball and tossed it toward the trash can. The shot hit the edge of the can, bounced onto the floor and rolled a few feet from him. With a sigh, he picked it up and dropped it into the trash can. Then he snagged his keys off the table and headed to the front door.

Had he lost his opportunity to tell Jenna how much he cared about her by not addressing his feelings after the kiss? He'd thought giving her space to process everything that happened was the considerate thing to do. Now he wasn't so sure.

Beau barked and raced after him. When they reached Sean's SUV, he opened the door and signaled Beau to hop in. "Let's go, Beau."

Sean wasn't sure where Jenna had gone, but he could not wait around for her to *be in touch*. She might or might not be open to a relationship, but he wouldn't know until he told her how he felt.

For the first time in three years, he felt fully alive, and he wasn't ready to give up on those feelings just yet.

"Lord, please give me the right words to say, and let her hear them with an open heart."

He climbed into his vehicle, reached into the glove compartment and pulled out Beau's restraint, then quickly fastened it on him and tethered him to the seat. Sean fastened his own seat belt and started the engine. "I'm not sure where we're headed, Beau. We may not even find her, but we have to try."

He would call her, but he suspected she'd send it to voicemail like she had yesterday. There was no other option but to drive around and try to find her. Even then, she might reject his affections. But he had to try. He'd lost so much in life already; he couldn't simply walk away from the woman who'd burrowed her way into his heart without at least letting her know what she meant to him.

"Okay, Beau, let's see if we can find Jenna and bring her *home*, where she belongs."

"I'll order the materials as soon as I leave here, and we'll get started on the repairs next week. Then, barring any unforeseen issues, we should have you back in your home in five or six weeks," Mr. Nabors closed the notebook he'd been making notes in and smiled at her.

"That sounds great." Jenna furrowed her brow. "I called my insurance company. They're supposed to send someone out to assess the damage and let me know what they're willing to pay."

Mr. Nabors, who was an old family friend of her parents', placed a hand on her shoulder. "Don't worry about it, dear. Whatever the insurance company won't cover, I will."

"I can't let—"

"Yes, you can. You've used your podcast to keep our community informed and safe for the past three years. It's our turn to give back to you." He pulled her into an embrace. "Call your parents before someone else notifies them of what's been going on here."

She smiled. "Yes, sir. Their plane should be landing within the hour. I'll text them to call me first thing."

"Good girl." He grinned and ambled down the porch steps.

The sound of Sean's vehicle approaching drew her attention, and she watched as he braked and turned into her drive, Beau sitting in the front passenger seat. The instant Sean opened his door, the coonhound jumped out and ran to her, howling as if he'd treed a wild animal.

"Looks like someone's happy to see you." Mr. Nabors laughed, shaking hands with Sean before climbing into his truck and backing out of the drive.

Jenna dropped to her knee and hugged the animal. "You act as if you haven't seen me in days, but I only left you an hour ago."

"It felt like an eternity." Sean stood at the foot of the steps, looking up at her. "Why did you leave without telling me goodbye?"

Swallowing the lump in her throat, she gave Beau one last hug and shoved to her feet. What could she say? That she had come to depend on him and the thought of not seeing him every day caused an unexpected ache in her heart? Her mom had always told her that when she faced something difficult, it was best to take care of it quickly to keep it from festering and becoming a bigger issue. Removing herself from his presence before her heart became even more invested in him and his loyal coonhound had seemed like the best way to protect herself.

When she was twenty-five years old and Patrick had walked out on her, Jenna had thought it was the end of the world. But she'd had to be strong for Becca, so she had persevered. Then she'd lost Becca and had experienced a pain unlike any other, one that had her spending days in bed, crying and gasping for air. At one point, she literally thought she was going to die from a broken heart. Only sheer determination and a desire to see Becca's murderer captured had kept her going.

She knew she was a capable woman, but she didn't know how many more heartaches her battered heart could stand. So she had to do whatever she could to protect it. If that meant walking away from a man who had made her wonder if there could be a happily-ever-after, so be it.

"I figured you were ready to get rid of me." She laughed. "Besides, when Mr. Nabors said he could meet me at the house this morning, I knew I needed to make it happen if I want back in my home quickly."

She turned, reached around the still-open front door, activated the lock and pulled it closed. "I was just headed to Hideaway Inn Bed and Breakfast. Mrs. Frances has a cabin I can rent until they complete the renovations on my house."

"There's no need for that. You're going to have enough expenses with the renovation. Stay at my house. I'll live in the camper."

"I can't let you do that. But I appreciate the neighborly offer." She brushed past him, but he captured her hand, halting her.

"I'm not being neighborly. I'm being selfish. I want to know you're safe, and I want to take care of you."

"Your responsibilities have ended. David is in jail. He can't hurt me anymore. Heath called and said the judge has denied bail." She bit her lip. "Tristan has agreed to testify against his father in exchange for his part in Becca's death being downgraded to misdemeanor manslaughter."

"I'm not surprised they've offered Tristan a plea deal. While I think he bears some of the responsibility for what happened, he trusted his father. Then his father convinced him that if he came forward at that point, no one would believe him." Sean tilted his head. "How do you feel about the plea deal?"

"I have mixed emotions. He was nineteen years old. He should've called someone, even if his dad said he would handle it. By the time he found out his dad hadn't called for help, Becca was already gone, and he was scared. I feel if he were truly evil, he would've ignored what his father was doing to me, and I wouldn't be alive right now. So I'm okay with the plea deal. I just hope that after he serves his prison time, he will come out and do good in the world." She met Sean's eyes. "I also selfishly hope that he'll choose somewhere else to live. I'm not sure how I feel about the possibility of running into him at the grocery store."

"That's understandable."

"Anyway." She shook her head. "Your responsibility to protect me is over. So, thank you, and maybe if you're up to it after I'm back in the house, you might stop in for coffee sometime." She turned and headed toward her rental vehicle. *Keep walking. Don't let him see you cry.*

"Hey, Jenna," Sean called after her. "What about your responsibility to me?"

Her steps faltered, and she turned hesitantly. "What do you mean?"

He looked her in the eyes and walked toward her unhurriedly. "What about...*your*...responsibility to me?"

"Oh," she gasped. "You're right, I should give you some money for the groceries and things. My wallet's in m—"

"I don't want your money. I want to know what you're

going to do to repair my broken heart. Since you're responsible for breaking it."

"I...uh..." She inhaled deeply, then released the breath slowly to the count of ten and willed her heart rate to slow. "How...?"

Sean reached up and pushed a strand of hair away from her face. "Did you think the kiss meant nothing?"

"I thought it just happened. That it was a sign of relief that everything was over." A tear slipped out of the corner of her eye, and he wiped it away. "That I was alive."

"Oh, it was all of those, but it was also pure joy and love. A love that I never knew I could have again." He smiled. "I have experienced relief over a case being solved and a witness staying alive, but I've never kissed any of them or even thought about it."

What was he saying? Did he care about her as she did him?

Lord, am I getting my happily-ever-after, after all these years?

"Jenna," Sean said softly, pressing the palm of his hand against her cheek. "I don't know the exact moment it happened. Maybe it was when I carried you out of the fire. Maybe it was when I found your note telling me you had gone to meet Tristan and I was so afraid I had lost you forever. Or maybe it was one of a million moments in between. All I know is that I have fallen for you. And I don't want to lose you."

Thank You, Lord. Tears streamed down her face, and she reached up and caressed his cheek. "I have fallen for you, too. But I was afraid to hope that you shared my feelings."

"Darling, Jenna, this is only the beginning. I will spend

the rest of my life making sure you know how much you are loved." As Beau barked and ran in circles around them, Sean lowered his head and claimed her lips.

Thank You, Lord, for sending this man to me and for new beginnings.

EPILOGUE

As he made his way up the walkway to Jenna's front door, Sean shifted the bouquet of red roses into his left hand and slipped his right hand into his suit-jacket pocket, needing reassurance the velvet ring box was still safely tucked inside. His heart raced. He prayed he'd get the response he was looking for, though he was sure Jenna's initial response would be concern for what other people would think about getting married after only dating for a short while.

He'd decided he didn't care much for what other people thought. If the last few years had taught him anything, it was that life was too short. Sean loved Jenna and wanted to spend the rest of his life with her. He didn't want to delay the start of their forever simply because a few people might think they were rushing things, and he prayed Jenna would see it the same way.

Taking the steps two at a time, he bounded onto the porch. The front door flew open as he reached out to press the doorbell.

"You're here." Jenna looked beautiful. She wore a flowy, royal blue dress with a pink-and-white floral print apron on top of it, but it was her smile that took his breath away.

She tilted her face upward, and he captured her lips in the sweetest kiss. The crinkling sound of cellophane alerted him to the flowers being crushed between them. He stepped back and held out the bouquet.

"These are beautiful. Thank you." She smiled and smelled the roses. "Let me put them in water."

Sean followed her inside and closed the door. He was immediately assaulted by the aroma of comfort food coming from the kitchen. "Mmm, something smells good."

"I called your mother and got her recipes for all of your favorite foods."

"Meat loaf, loaded mashed potatoes, mac 'n' cheese, and…" He sniffed the air. "German chocolate cake."

Jenna laughed. "I hope you're hungry. It's been a long time since I've cooked a meal for two. I may have gone a little overboard."

He followed her into the kitchen. She opened a cabinet, pulled out a vase and filled it with water. After removing the cellophane wrapping from the flowers, she arranged them in the vase and carried them to the dining room table. The table had been set with a lace tablecloth, china place settings and candles. It looked elegant. A smile tugged the corners of his lips. He couldn't have planned a better setting for his proposal if he'd done all the work himself.

"You look happy."

"Oh, I am. Blissfully so." He captured her hand in his and pulled it to his lips.

He'd planned to wait until after dinner, but if Sean didn't propose right then, he felt as if he might burst. "Is everything on the stove fine for a few moments? I'd like to talk before dinner if that's okay."

She nodded. "Sure. We have about ten minutes before I have to take the meat loaf out of the oven."

Jenna led him to the living room sofa. Sitting in the room where he'd saved her from the burning inferno just seven short weeks ago sent a shudder up his spine. If he hadn't been driving along at that exact moment, there was a good chance she wouldn't have made it out alive.

"That's the same reaction I had when I sat in this room for the first time after the repairs. Mr. Nabors and his crew did a wonderful job on the remodel, but I can still see the events of that night clearly in my mind."

Sean squeezed her hand. "But you got out in time. That's the important thing."

"Because of you." Her smile widened. "Nurse Bethany was right. You, Sean Quinn, are my knight in shining armor."

As hard as he tried, he couldn't stop the laughter that flowed out of him, filling the room. "Don't tell me you're still jealous that Nurse Bethany flirted with me."

"Who…me?" She feigned shock and winked at him, a saucy twinkle in her eye. Then she joined in the laughter. Quickly sobering, she smiled. "I will never blame any woman for noticing how attractive you are, as long as they know you're mine."

"I'm glad you feel that way, because I—"

"Wait…please. I have something I want to say first." She licked her lips and smiled. "After my divorce, I was convinced I wasn't lovable."

"That's not—"

Jenna placed a finger on his lips, silencing him. "I now know that isn't true. I allowed someone else's opinion of me to become more important than my own opinion of myself. You have taught me to find the joy in every day. To embrace love. And to silence the naysayers."

Tears sparkled in her eyes. "I know you don't want to take credit for saving me, but we both know, if you hadn't been by my side, I would not be here today."

He opened his mouth to speak. But she shook her head, and he pressed his lips together. *Lord, when it's my turn to speak, help me find the words to let her know what a beautiful, loving woman she is.*

"I can't believe I'm saying this, but here goes." She puffed out a breath. "Sean, if you hadn't saved me, I wouldn't be alive. But being alive isn't enough. I love you, and I don't want to live without you." Tugging her hand free, she reached into the pocket of her apron and pulled out a small box.

His breath caught. Was she really doing what he thought she was doing? He slipped his hand into his own pocket and pulled out the velvet box he was carrying. When she caught sight of it, she giggled.

"On three?" she asked, beaming from ear to ear as she opened the small box she was holding, revealing a white-gold band with a carved infinity-symbol design.

He nodded, opening the velvet box to reveal the one-carat oval-cut diamond set in white gold. "One…two…three!"

"Sean Quinn, will you marry me?"

"Marry me, Jenna Hartley!"

"Yes!" they said in unison.

"I love you." He swept Jenna into his arms and kissed her. *Thank You, Lord, for entrusting me with this woman's heart. I promise to cherish her, all the days of my life.*

* * * * *

Dear Reader,

Thank you for reading Sean and Jenna's story of love and forgiveness. I hope you enjoyed it. Writing their story reminded me that everyone handles grief differently. Some rely on God for strength and comfort and surround themselves with family and friends. Others choose to shut everyone out, even, sometimes, God. Once Jenna found her way back to God, she was able to open her heart to love and a happily-ever-after with Sean.

Grief never truly goes away, and there will always be an emptiness where a loved one once was. However, as Jenna and Sean discovered, turning to God allows Him to carry us during our darkest times. God's love is unwavering.

I would love to hear from you. Please connect with me at www.rhondastarnes.com or follow me on Facebook @ AuthorRhondaStarnes.

All my best,
Rhonda Starnes